Her breathing was coming faster now. His blood had thickened and slowed. She was all heat, enticing curves, and endless temptation. He inhaled sharply as pleasure slammed through his body and knotted in his loins. He heard her faintly moan. As far as he was concerned, this kiss was only the beginning of what he wanted from her.

Then she stiffened and pressed her palms against his shoulders. She wanted to end what she had started, he thought wryly. Too bad, because he wasn't quite ready. If she didn't know it already, she needed to learn that it was dangerous to start a game with a stranger.

Besides, she fit against him as if she had been made for him and she tasted of everything he craved. He wanted to explore the promise of what could happen between the two of them if he held her just a little longer, kissed her more thoroughly.

She made a sound and pushed harder against him.

With a muffled curse, he released her.

"Who are you?"

"It doesn't matter," she said breathlessly. She swirled and ran.

"Wait!" He started after her, but then stopped as a surge of quick, hot anger hit him with the force of a fist to his gut. She was running toward a young man who was holding a small video camera.

WHAT ARE *LOVESWEPT* ROMANCES?

They are stories of true romance and touching emotion. We believe those two very important ingredients are constants in our highly sensual and very believable stories in the LOVE- SWEPT line. Our goal is to give you, the reader, stories of consistently high quality that may sometimes make you laugh, sometimes make you cry, but are always fresh and creative and contain many delightful surprises within their pages.

Most romance fans read an enormous number of books. Those they truly love, they keep. Others may be traded with friends and soon forgotten. We hope that each LOVESWEPT romance will be a treasure—a "keeper." We will always try to publish

LOVE STORIES YOU'LL NEVER FORGET
BY AUTHORS YOU'LL ALWAYS REMEMBER

The Editors

The Damaron Mark:

THE
PRIZE

FAYRENE
PRESTON

BANTAM BOOKS
NEW YORK · TORONTO · LONDON · SYDNEY · AUCKLAND

THE DAMARON MARK: THE PRIZE

A Bantam Book / December 1998

ISBN 0-553-44536-7

Published simultaneously in the United States and Canada

Bantam Books are published by Bantam Books, a division of Bantam Doubleday Dell Publishing Group, Inc. Its trademark, consisting of the words "Bantam Books" and the portrayal of a rooster, is Registered in U.S. Patent and Trademark Office and in other countries. Marca Registrada. Bantam Books, 1540 Broadway, New York, New York 10036.

PRINTED IN THE UNITED STATES OF AMERICA

OPM   10 9 8 7 6 5 4 3 2 1

To Jacquelyn Ralls Forcher,
an extraordinary and gracious
dancer and teacher

ONE

A *bateau-mouche* glided over the dark water of the Seine. The glow from the lamplight joined the silvery light of the moon to dance on the spreading wake.

It had been a long day, Nathan Damaron reflected, casually slipping his hands into his pockets as he strolled along the rough stones of the quay. But Paris never disappointed. The city was like a beautiful woman, seductive in her diamond lights and intriguing scents. Spring was in the air and lovers were in each other's arms.

"Excuse me?"

A young woman materialized in front of him. So suddenly had she appeared, he was instantly forced to halt before he walked right into her. He caught sight of a lovely face, long brown hair, and a smile.

"Would you mind kissing me as if you're madly in love with me and are never going to let me go?"

she asked in a rush. Without waiting for his answer, she threw her arms around his neck and pressed her lips to his.

Instantly, he grabbed her upper arms, intending to untangle them from around his neck and push her away, but before he could, his body took control over his mind. Her lips were closed. Still, there was something especially alluring about her. He had no idea who she was, but he'd never been a man to pass up an opportunity, whether it was a good business deal or an exquisitely lovely woman.

Sure, he'd go along. Why not?

He wrapped his arms around her waist and pulled her against him so that her soft breasts crushed against his chest and her slim body pressed the length of his. He hadn't known how she'd react. Didn't care, really. But she tensed.

Strange that she hadn't been prepared for the consequences of her actions. Even so, he kept his movements deliberately gentle. Despite the fact that she'd instigated their encounter, he didn't want her to feel threatened, nor did he want her to panic, but he *did* want more.

He moved his lips back and forth over hers until he felt her body begin slowly, almost imperceptibly, to relax, and her lips began to part, tentatively, sweetly. Still, he was careful not to go too quickly.

But her lips were soft and tasted of honey and he had every intention of taking this kiss further. He lifted his mouth briefly, then brought it down on hers from another angle. Heat wound its way through him as he felt her body flow into his.

Her breathing was coming faster now. His blood had thickened and slowed. He could feel the points of her stiffened nipples against his chest and longed to take her breast into his hand. However, they were in public and he had to satisfy himself in another way.

He slid his fingers upward through her astonishingly silky hair until he was cupping her head, then he thrust his tongue deep into her mouth.

Once again, she responded, softening, opening. She smelled of flowers and beguiling femininity. As slight as she was, she fit perfectly against him. She was all heat, enticing curves, and endless temptation. He inhaled sharply as pleasure slammed through his body and knotted in his loins. He heard her faintly moan. As far as he was concerned, whoever she was, whatever she wanted, this kiss was only the beginning of what he wanted from her.

Then she stiffened and pressed her palms against his shoulders. She wanted to end what she had started, he thought wryly. Too bad, because he wasn't quite ready. If she didn't know it already, she needed to learn that it was dangerous to start a game with a stranger without any guarantee of how he would react or what direction he might take the game.

Besides, she fit against him as if she had been made for him and she tasted of everything he craved. He wanted to explore the promise of what could happen between the two of them if he held her just a little longer, kissed her more thoroughly.

She made a sound and pushed harder against him.

With a muffled curse, he released her. He would have much rather continued the kiss, but he was also more than ready to find out her name and the reason for her decidedly unconventional methods. But astonishingly, as he looked down into her eyes, he saw shock and wariness. Why? Surely she must have thought out her actions before she threw herself at him.

"Who are you?"

"It doesn't matter," she said breathlessly. "Thank you for your cooperation." She swirled and ran.

"Wait!" He started after her, but then stopped as a surge of quick, hot anger hit him with the force of a fist to his gut. She was running toward a young man who was holding a small video camera. As she approached the next set of stone steps that led to the walkway above, the young man caught her hand and hurriedly pulled her up the steps. Then they were gone.

He blew out a long, calming breath, steadying himself. Obviously the young man was her partner and had taped the entire kiss. There was no potential in blackmail there—they'd only gotten a picture of a single man kissing a pretty girl. But that didn't matter. He knew all too well how the tabloids could spin a story out of air.

Years ago, when he and his cousins had inherited their family's business, they had made a policy to refuse all interviews regarding their personal lives. It hadn't mattered, though. They had long been a treasure trove for tabloids and popular magazines to mine. Undaunted by a family who zealously guarded their privacy, the newsprint publishers made do with the candid pictures they could get and the text they made up.

And money slipped to a bellman or a maid would ensure their knowledge of which Damaron was in what city. In this case, he and his cousins Sin and Lion were in Paris to conduct business meetings concerning several of the Damaron European holdings. They had one more meeting scheduled tonight, a dinner meeting in thirty minutes back at their hotel.

Sin and Lion had used this short break to go up to their suite to call their wives, but he'd seized the time to get out of the hotel. He hadn't been tired, but he'd definitely felt the need to grab a breath of fresh air and take a walk. A glimpse of the City of Light, he'd figured, would be an added benefit.

Slowly, he smiled. He certainly hadn't counted on being stopped and kissed by a lovely young woman.

Normally he was able to avoid the paparazzi, but in this case, he'd been set up and set up masterfully. If selling the tape was truly what the girl and her partner had in mind, then they would be very sorry. It didn't matter what publication or even television magazine show the video ended up in, he'd still be able to find out who she was. If the head of the company wouldn't willingly give him the name of the person from whom they'd bought the tape, he'd send his entire legal department over to the offices. If suing the company didn't work, then he'd buy the damn place.

And then . . . His smile broadened in anticipation. When he did . . . Well, he'd play it by ear. But one way or another, he would see the woman again.

Rare Siena marble, heavy silk draperies, Aubusson rugs, and gold-leafed woodwork met Danielle Savourat's gaze as she walked into the Hôtel Crillon, but there was no sign of the person she was there to see.

A glance at her watch told her it was a bit late for dinner, but she still checked the Ambassadors Salon. He wasn't there either. Her nervousness increased. Over the phone, the hotel wouldn't confirm that he was registered there, but it made sense that he was. One way or the other, she planned to find out. If he wasn't here, she'd go on to the next hotel and the next. She had to find him and she needed to do it tonight or she might lose her nerve.

She got lucky. In the doorway of the hotel's bar, L'Obélisque, she paused and gazed toward the man she'd been looking for.

Hindsight was a wonderful thing and, in this

case, absolutely useless to her. In the hours since she'd last seen him, she'd learned she should have taken a better look at him before she'd rushed up and thrown her arms around him. If she'd seen that silver streak in his hair, she would *never* have chosen him to kiss.

Very few people in the world carried a silver streak like the one he had. It marked him as a Damaron. Now that she was looking at him again, she didn't know how she'd missed it. The silver streak was remarkable for its prominence in his dark brown hair. Perhaps when she'd first seen him, that part of his head had been in shadows. Or maybe she'd made her decision too fast after catching a glance at his face.

Dumb, Dani. Very, very dumb.

But in that first glance, she'd received an impression of intelligence and strength, not to mention the fact that he was incredibly nice-looking. Truthfully, he'd been the first person she'd seen all night whom she wouldn't mind kissing. In fact, not in the least.

So she'd kissed him and nearly lost herself in his arms. Belatedly, but thankfully, she'd remembered that Kevin was waiting for her and getting the entire kiss on tape. Flustered by her response, she'd pulled away and run.

But when she and Kevin had gotten back to the apartment and shown their tape, her friends, with irritatingly great glee, had identified him for her as Nathan Damaron.

Worse than dumb, Dani. Incredibly stupid.

She put her hand on her stomach where it felt as if a big glob of cement had taken form. Her skin was cold and clammy. If she wasn't mistaken, a tension headache was beginning to constrict her scalp. There weren't too many things that made her nervous, but then she'd never before had to apologize to a Damaron.

And just her luck, there wasn't one Damaron at the table, there were *three*.

What, she wondered, did one call two or more Damarons? A gaggle? A flock? A herd? No. She had it. *A power convergence*.

Not that it mattered. Not that it changed the ordeal that was before her by a whit. She was only killing time.

She braced herself. She knew what she had to do and she wouldn't be able to rest until she'd done it. Slowly she walked toward the table, keeping her eye on the smile Nathan was directing at his cousins.

"Excuse me."

Nathan's head snapped up and she found herself the recipient of a hard, gray-eyed gaze, startling and sharp enough to shatter all the stone statues across Paris. The other two Damarons merely gazed curiously at her.

"Yes?" one them asked.

"I'm sorry to bother you all, but I need to speak with Nathan." She glanced at the two, but returned her gaze to him, and nearly lost her train of thought.

He had a strong face with a square jaw and full lips. It hadn't been that long since those lips had been on hers. His kiss had rocked her to her toes. If she hadn't come to her senses and broken it off, she had the feeling he would still be kissing her. And she would still be reveling in it. In retrospect, she knew she would never have approached him if she'd given herself time to think, or even looked at him twice.

She swallowed. "That is, if you don't mind." She clasped her hands together. "And actually even if you do, I still need to speak with you."

Nathan leaned back in his chair, his expression cold and hostile. "Ah, the lady of the kiss and the video camera. I didn't think I'd hear from you this soon."

"You thought you'd hear from me?"

"Of course. I just didn't know how, and I must say, I honestly didn't think you'd contact me in person—*and* alone. You must be very brave. Or very stupid."

Stupid, she thought wearily. No question about it. She'd already admitted it to herself, but she could definitely have done without *him* calling her stupid. "Look, I came because—"

He glanced over her shoulder, then back at her. "Where's your boyfriend?"

She was already embarrassed to be in the position of having to seek him out, but she'd never expected to be thoroughly confused as well.

"My boyfriend?" she repeated. Then it hit her.

"Oh, you must have seen Kevin. He's a friend, not my boyfriend."

"I wouldn't think he's much of a friend if he let you come here alone."

She glanced at the other two Damarons and discovered their demeanor had suddenly turned as hard as Nathan's. Obviously they'd picked up on their cousin's caustic mood, and now they looked as if they would behead her in the blink of an eye if their cousin indicated she'd hurt him in some way. Perhaps she was exaggerating the matter to herself, but even if she wasn't, this encounter wasn't going at all as she'd planned. She'd thought she'd simply say her piece and then leave. Instead, Nathan had taken charge of the conversation and, with his questions, was leading her down a path she knew nothing about.

"There was no reason for Kevin to come. This has nothing to do with him."

"So he was just an unwitting accomplice?"

She shifted her weight from one foot to the other. "He wasn't an unwitting anything. We were a team, and he was there to tape what was happening."

"Yeah, so I noticed." He studied her for a moment. "How did you know where to find me?"

"Well, it's just that this is the closest palace to where . . ."

Her voice trailed off as she realized her little attempt at a joke had fallen flat. She'd heard the Damaron family called American royalty before.

Surely they'd heard the same thing. The Hôtel Crillon had formerly been a palace, built for Louis XV. Royalty. Palace. It had seemed funny to her, but her little attempt at breaking the ice fell flat. Instead of cracking jokes, she counseled herself, she should concentrate on accomplishing what she'd come for, then getting out with her skin still intact.

"The Hôtel Crillon is the closest exclusive, high-priced hotel to the place where—" She stopped again, this time for a different reason, and cleared her throat. "Where—"

"Where you threw yourself at me and kissed me," he supplied, his tone helpful, his expression anything but.

At the second mention of a kiss, the attitude of the other two Damarons changed slightly. Now they seemed more interested than hostile. With a glance at each other, they settled back in their chairs, obviously having no intention of going anywhere.

Danielle passed her fingers across her forehead. She could feel her face growing hot with embarrassment. "Look. If I can just have a private word with you, I'll explain everything."

Nathan shook his head. "My cousins and I don't keep secrets from one another. Besides, if they don't find out about it now, they'll find out about it when I bring our legal department in on this."

Danielle felt the color drain from her face. "Legal department?"

"What did you expect? Paparazzi are very unpopular these days, plus if you plan to sell your tape to a tabloid—"

Her mouth nearly fell open. "*Sell the tape?* I have no intention of selling it."

"Surely you don't think you can blackmail me. It was only a kiss."

Only a kiss. Right, she reflected. If that had been only a kiss, then the *Mona Lisa* was only a painting. "Of course *not*."

Abruptly the cousin with the jade-colored eyes stood. "I'm afraid our manners have been severely lacking. I'm Sinclair Damaron," he said. "This is my cousin Lion." Lion nodded to her.

"How do you do." She gave Sinclair a grateful smile and extended her hand. "I'm Danielle Savourat."

He held an empty chair out for her. "Please sit. I don't know about my cousins, but I'm getting a crick in my neck from having to look up at you."

She sat, thankful for the chair, because somewhere along the line, her legs had become weak.

"I gather you already know Nathan," Sinclair said, taking his seat.

"In a manner of speaking." She cast a wary glance his way.

A waitress glided up to the table. "May I get you something to drink?"

She rarely drank, and she'd certainly never been one to resort to alcohol for courage, but in this case, she decided she'd take it any way she could get it. "I'll have whatever they're having."

"Good choice," Sin said. "We're having Napoléon brandy. You'll never taste anything smoother."

Dani nearly choked. There was no way she could afford even a single glass of the stuff. "On second thought," she said to the waitress, "I don't want anything. Thank you, anyway."

"Are you sure?" Sin asked.

She nodded, then smiled. "I just remembered I'm allergic to anything alcoholic."

Lion and Sin looked at her oddly.

"Gentlemen, do you need refills?" the waitress asked. The three men shook their heads and the waitress departed.

Danielle smiled at Sinclair again. "Thank you for the introductions. I wasn't certain of your names." Her gaze slid to Nathan. "Except for yours, and I only knew after some friends told me."

"It's generally enough for a blackmailer or a member of the paparazzi to know they have a Damaron in the crosshairs of their camera," Nathan said. "They find out our names later, just as you did."

Lion nodded. "But you're unique. I don't think we've ever had either of those type of people come up to us and introduce themselves."

"It's definitely a novel approach," Sin agreed, his tone vaguely sympathetic, "but I have to tell you that you're going to be no more successful than the blackmailers who have come before you."

"People try, but one way or another, we always stop them," Lion added

She glanced at Nathan. He was silently watching her, his gaze still hard, but now she thought she saw something else there. Thoughtfulness. It was as if his initial anger with her was slowly dissolving into assessment. Lord, he was really something to look at. No wonder she'd chosen him to kiss. He was wearing a navy tweed jacket over a dark blue shirt, opened at the throat, and she could feel herself involuntarily softening as she remembered how right it had felt when he'd held her in his arms.

"Of course," Lion said, "none of the blackmailers have been as pretty as you are, but if I were you, I'd concentrate on a tabloid sell. It would be much easier for you."

That did it. She'd had enough. She put up her hands, palms out. "Okay, *stop. Both* of you. And just listen to me. I appreciate your primer on the dos and don'ts of blackmailing and selling to a tabloid. Career advice is always valuable. Who knows? One day I might have need of it. However, that's not why I'm here." She looked at Nathan. "I came here for one reason—to apologize to you."

Lion nodded with approval. "Once again, a fresh approach."

She flashed him a glance of rebuke. "Be quiet. I need to get this out. Unfortunately, I didn't take into account that I'd have to deal with *three* of you—"

"You'll often find us in packs," Sin offered, then when she sent a cutting look his way, he shrugged.

"Just thought you'd like to know for any future plans."

She sighed. "Obviously you two took my arrival as your evening's entertainment, but I have something very important to say to Nathan, and if either one of you says one more word, I'll dump that two-hundred-year-old brandy on your head."

Sin's dark brows shot up and Lion's golden eyes narrowed. "At least I'd give it my best try," she amended. "Now . . ." She directed her attention to Nathan. "As I said before, my name is Danielle Savourat. My father is Édouard Savourat. Before his retirement, he and his company, United Electronics, did a great deal of business with Damaron International."

"Oh, you're Édouard's daughter," Lion said. "He's a good man."

"Thank you." She looked back at Nathan. "So when I realized that the man I'd kissed on the quay was a Damaron, I knew I had to come and apologize. Even though my father has retired and no longer does business with you and your family, he would be quite upset at my behavior this evening."

She paused, but she couldn't tell if her words had any effect on Nathan. But it was all right. She'd accomplished what she'd come to do. "So that's it. Again, I'm very, very sorry, and I can assure you it will never happen again." She pushed away from the table, but before she could stand, Nathan's voice stopped her.

"Just a minute. You haven't told me *why* you did it."

She drew in a deep breath, then nodded. "Okay. You deserve to know that. There was nothing nefarious or mercenary about my actions. I was simply on a scavenger hunt."

Lion shook his head in admiration. "Once again, I have to give it to you, Danielle. There's certainly nothing clichéd or hackneyed about you."

She ignored him and kept her gaze on Nathan. "I had a group of very close friends during school, and when we graduated, we vowed we'd always stay close. So once a year we try our best to gather together somewhere for however long we can manage. This year, as it happened, two of our friends have been living here, so we decided we'd all come to Paris and bunk in with them."

She glanced at Sin and Lion and saw that they had relaxed back in their chairs and were listening with great enjoyment. She returned her gaze to Nathan, who, unfortunately, hadn't relaxed at all. "So last night, we decided to have a scavenger hunt. There were a lot of crazy things on our list. You know, like a bow from a poodle's ear, or a Maxim's menu autographed by the maître d', which by the way, was very hard to get. Another hard one involved willpower—a *whole* freshly baked chocolate éclair. It couldn't be eaten until we all got back to the apartment and after the prize had been awarded. Oh, and a picture of a dog eating a T-bone from fine china on the floor at a restaurant. Surprisingly, that wasn't hard at all to get. Ummm . . . a picture of one of us riding atop an equestrian statue. That wasn't hard either. There are so many of them in this city. It was just a matter of finding one without a gendarme in the area." She shrugged. "As I said, silly things. And to keep us all legal, each team of two had to videotape the other getting the object."

"Object?"

She shifted uncomfortably in her seat. "Or thing, such as a kiss from a stranger. My teammate, Kevin, is engaged to a girl back in the States, so he said I had to do that part." Something flickered in Nathan's eyes, so she rushed on. "We already had a lot of the items on the list and our time was running out. That's when I saw you. I got the kiss from you and then we ran back to the apartment and managed to arrive just minutes before the deadline was up." She shrugged again. "And that was pretty much it."

"Not quite. Did you win?"

She shifted in her chair. "As a matter of fact we did. We were tied with two other teams, but when we ran our tape and, uh, everyone saw me kiss you, they decided Kevin and I had won hands down."

"And why's that?"

"Because they noticed what I didn't." She nodded toward his head. "The silver streak in your hair. My friends immediately recognized you. Many of them had gotten kisses from strangers, but no one had managed to get a kiss from someone famous."

Sin glanced at Lion. "Just think of the confusion we could have caused if we'd gone out. Ties, wins—they would have been up all night trying to figure out who topped who."

Lion grinned. "What criteria do you suppose they would have used to declare the winner then? Perhaps who kissed the oldest Damaron?"

"Or maybe who kissed the best-looking?"

Lion flashed a dazzling smile. "That would be me, of course."

"Not on your longest day."

She liked Sin and Lion, she decided. Too bad their cousin didn't appear to see the humor in the situation as they did. "There was only one thing that would have beaten the kiss from Nathan," she said to the two of them.

Lion grinned. "Oh, I can't wait to hear this one."

"The *real* hunchback of Notre Dame."

Sin and Lion burst out laughing.

"What was the prize?" Nathan asked quietly.

"The prize?"

"What did you win because you kissed me?"

"An Eiffel Tower snow globe."

"I beg your pardon?"

Her brow pleated as she looked at him. "It's a glass ball that holds snowlike flakes and, in this case, the Eiffel Tower. Turn it upside down, then right-side up again, and it snows on the Eiffel Tower."

Lion's eyes glittered with laughter. "I for one am impressed. Think about it, Nathan. You're worth a snow globe. I don't know of many people who could say that."

Sin laughed, then glanced at his watch and nudged Lion. "I almost forgot. You and I have a conference call coming in from Geneva. We'd better go up to the suite."

Lion frowned. "Conference call?"

"Yes," Sin said meaningfully. "From Geneva. For you and me. Not Nathan."

Lion glanced at Nathan. "Oh—*right*. Now I remember. Conference call from Geneva. You. Me. Not Nathan."

"It was very nice meeting you, Danielle," Sin said, standing.

Lion also rose to his feet. "And *very* interesting."

Smiling, Danielle nodded. "It was nice meeting you too." After the two men left, she returned her gaze to Nathan. "I'll be going too. Once again, I'm very sorry. My father has always thought a great deal of you and your cousins. When he was doing business with Damaron International, he constantly sang your praises. He greatly admired the way you and your cousins took over the business after your parents' deaths. That's just one of the reasons I wouldn't want anything I did to reflect badly on him."

"Don't worry about that. I know your father. He's a man of integrity."

"Yes, he is." She smiled at him. "Thank you for saying so. Well . . . good night."

She put her hands on the table to push herself up, but he reached across the table and grabbed her wrist. "Stay."

"I've said everything I have to say."

"But I haven't."

TWO

Even though Nathan had felt he would see her again, he hadn't expected it would be so soon and under these circumstances. But he was glad that she'd come, and that the man she'd been with hadn't been her boyfriend after all. He was equally glad and relieved that she hadn't turned out to be a con artist. Not that either of those things would have ultimately mattered to him.

He knew her name now. Danielle. And she was even more lovely than he'd been able to see down on the quay. She had misty blue eyes and long, light brown hair. If he'd seen her walking on the quay, she would have attracted his attention. If she'd smiled at him, as she had a minute or so ago, he would have been captivated.

He'd been smiled at by many beautiful women, but there was something unique about Danielle.

Very few things he could think of would have

gained her his complete and undivided attention as quickly as the kiss had. It had been a sucker punch. He hadn't seen it coming, and when it did arrive, he'd been helpless to guard against it.

He'd been thinking about it ever since.

He'd looked forward to their next encounter, because he'd thought he would be able to make her pay for kissing him as she had, for making him want her, then for running away with another man.

But she'd foiled him.

"Isn't a scavenger hunt kids' play?"

"I suppose it depends on your point of view. My friends and I thought it was great fun, and we didn't break too many laws."

"Too many?"

She shrugged. "More importantly, no one got hurt."

"I suppose that depends on your point of view."

"You're talking about the kiss, aren't you?"

"That *was* the only part of the scavenger hunt I was personally involved in."

Firmly she shook her head, causing her hair to ripple over her shoulders. "You weren't hurt, Nathan. I didn't leave one mark on you, inside or out."

He smiled inwardly. She'd been nervous when she'd first arrived, but around the time she'd told Sin and Lion to stop talking and listen—something very few people had ever done, but something he knew they'd gotten a kick out of—she'd come into her own. She had backbone and seemingly every bit as much integrity as her father.

Since Édouard was retired, he probably would never have known what she'd done unless she'd told him. But her sense of rightness had brought her here to apologize.

"In fact, you probably wouldn't have even remembered the kiss if I hadn't showed up again."

"You're wrong, but never mind that now. Let's talk more about the kiss."

A slight wariness crept into her expression. "What about it?"

"Do you often go around kissing strange men?"

She sighed. "It was a *game*, Nathan. Don't you ever play games?"

"Quite often. But I've never kissed a strange woman, especially without warning."

"I gave you warning."

He smiled. "Of a sort. By the way, what made you choose me?"

He saw her gaze drop to his smile and felt a surge of satisfaction. She wasn't unaffected by him.

"Quite honestly, it was fairly simple. I hadn't made the decision yet to go for that particular item on our list, but when I saw you, you looked like someone I wouldn't mind kissing, and I went for it."

"Someone you wouldn't mind kissing," he repeated slowly.

"Look. It was never intended to be a big deal. It was only supposed to be a closed-mouth kiss and it wasn't supposed to last long. It was you who—"

"Opened your mouth and kept you longer than

you intended? Don't blame me, Danielle. I was only following your orders."

"*My* orders?"

He nodded. "You said, 'Kiss me as if you're madly in love with me and are never going to let me go.' "

"Right, I did." She grimaced. "Those words just sort of popped out. I'm not sure why."

"Okay, then, what was it about me that made you think I'd go along with you?"

She fixed him with a look of exasperation. "You could have taught the people involved in the Spanish Inquisition something about interrogation. What are you going to do next? Put me on the rack?"

"Not if you answer my question."

She leaned forward and propped her forearms on the table. "I know you and your family have had to guard against a lot of people who have wanted to harm you, but please believe me when I say that kissing you tonight was not part of some Byzantine plot on my part. I was simply running around Paris, having fun with my friends, nothing more, nothing less. As for the kiss, I chose you because I thought you were nice-looking, and I figured if I took you off guard by saying what I did, and I kissed you fast enough, you wouldn't have a chance to turn me down."

There was a sweetness in her effort to reassure him, and he realized with vague surprise that she had touched him on some emotional level. "As it turns out, you didn't need to catch me off guard. I rarely turn down a request from a beautiful woman."

She sat back and eyed him consideringly. "You must stay very busy."

He smiled. "I keep myself occupied. Tell me about yourself."

Once again, she stared at his smile for a moment. "I don't see the point. I've done what I came here to do. Now I should really get back to my friends."

"Not yet. Not until you pay me what you owe me."

"Excuse me?" She looked stunned. "You think I *owe* you something?"

"Yes, I do. You said it yourself. You won because of who I am. I helped you to win your prize, your snow globe. In my book, that means you owe me."

"That's ridiculous."

"Is that what your father would say?"

"Are you saying you'll tell my father if I don't pay you back?"

"If I ever threaten you, Danielle," he said softly, "you won't have to ask. You'll know."

She exhaled a long breath. "You're not talking about money, are you?"

He stared at her for several moments. A game had been behind the kiss, chance had been behind her choosing him, but it didn't matter. The kiss had happened, and though she might not want to admit it, they'd connected during the kiss. She might be willing to let it go at that, but he wasn't.

"I have a charity ball to attend in New York in three days, but I don't have a date yet. You're going to come with me."

She looked at him blankly. "Me?"

He nodded.

"But why? There must be scores of women who would love to be your date."

"That's not the point, is it? The point is that because of me, you won the prize. You owe me and this is how I want you to repay me."

"And you wouldn't be just as happy with a snow globe?" she suggested tentatively.

He smiled, fully, and with humor. "No snow globe."

"I see," she said as she sat there absorbing his smile and feeling something shift in her. Technically, in the strictest sense of the word, she supposed he was right. She'd admitted to him that he had helped her win the game, which, for some reason, he'd decided meant she owed him. Now he was calling in the debt. Who knew why?

She'd gone on a scavenger hunt and found a Damaron, and now she appeared to be stuck with him for a little while longer. She knew there were people who would say she was the luckiest girl in the world, but she wasn't so sure. "You say I owe you. That must mean you're upset with me in some way."

"Not now."

"But you were."

He nodded. "When I thought you were going to sell the tape, I was very angry. But now I know you were simply using me in an entirely different way that had only a small part to do with money."

"Money?"

"It took money to buy the snow globe, right, so therefore it's worth money, even if it cost only a few francs."

She wasn't certain she believed him when he said he was no longer angry with her, she reflected as she tried to reason her way through his motive. True, what she'd done had been a bit outrageous. Oh, okay, it had been a lot outrageous. And also true, the kiss had been more than she had bargained for and so had he. She remembered the kiss as if it had happened moments instead of hours ago.

"You owe me, Danielle. The snow globe is proof of that."

"And what would you do if I refused to go along with you on this?"

To her astonishment, his eyes began to twinkle and a shiver ran down her spine. This man was dangerous on many levels.

"Oh, come on, Danielle. You don't really want to find that out, do you?"

He was being completely charming now, but she couldn't miss the steel behind the words.

He went on. "It's not as if I'm asking you to give me your last dime, is it? Or even do something as outrageous as strip naked right here and now and have sex with me on this table."

His hand flattened on the table and her heart gave a leap. It was a big hand, with long fingers and fine dark hair on its back. She remembered how he'd cupped her head and thrust his tongue deep into her mouth. The kiss had almost undone her. What would having sex with him to do her?

"Danielle? This can't be that hard a decision for you."

By rights, it shouldn't be. He was one of the most eligible men in the world and he was simply asking her to attend a ball with him. Why was she hesitating? With her next breath she answered herself. Because with him she had a feeling there was nothing *simple* about anything he did. "When did you say this ball was?" she asked carefully.

"Three days from now. This Saturday."

Relieved, she shook her head. "I'm not due to return to New York until Sunday. My plane leaves Saturday afternoon."

"Your plans can be changed."

"No, I'm sorry, but they can't. My friends and I got the cheapest fares we could. Our flight plans are locked in and there is no refund."

"Your father is Édouard Savourat. Money *can't* be an issue."

"I stopped taking money from my father the day I graduated from college. I pay my own way in everything I do."

He stared at her for a moment, then shook his

head. "Well, in any event, this is no problem. You can fly home with me."

"I'm sorry, but I can't afford another ticket and I won't allow you to buy one for me."

He smiled, revealing a row of even, white teeth that reminded her of a shark's. "I don't have to. My jet will be flying back to New York tomorrow afternoon. I'll be on it, and it won't cost a cent more if you're aboard."

She almost groaned. "You have your own plane?" Of course he did. "Will your cousins be aboard too?" Maybe it wouldn't be too bad if Sinclair and Lion were with them. She liked them.

"No, they'll be flying home in their own separate planes. We try not to fly together unless it's absolutely necessary."

"Right." She remembered now. It was a policy formed because of their parents' deaths. Her thoughts returned to his request. There was no getting around it, he had an answer for everything.

Her father had always told her that a person who crossed a Damaron would regret it for the rest of his life. But he had also told her that if a person was fair and honest, that Damaron would be fair and honest with him. That thought was what was keeping her in her seat. She'd started the game. He was asking her only to finish it out.

Truthfully, he'd be a hard man for any woman to turn down. He was a man of great power and charm and the ability to kiss a woman until she forgot and went much further than she'd intended.

With her, it had started with the kiss, and here it was, happening again. She wanted to go to the ball with him.

She met his gaze. "Never let it be said that I don't pay my debts. And since we'll be attending a ball together, call me Dani."

He slowly smiled. "Dani."

By the time she returned to the apartment, her friends had already crashed for the night. She threaded her way across a floor full of sleeping bodies and made it to the bathroom. There, she undressed, washed up, and finally, in a T-shirt and boxer shorts, slipped into her own sleeping bag.

"Dani?" she heard her friend Marcia whisper.

She rolled over to face her. "Yeah?" she whispered back.

"How'd it go?"

"Somewhere between the Spanish Inquisition and a meat grinder."

"Hey, at least you're back in one piece."

"I'm not so sure."

"Why?"

"He wants me to fly back with him on his private jet tomorrow and attend a ball Saturday night."

"Hey, way to go. Sounds like you caught yourself a Damaron."

"I don't think so. It's more like he caught me."

❖━━━❖

There was a subtle grace about Dani, even while she slept, Nathan reflected as he watched her. They hadn't really talked since they'd boarded the jet in Paris. As was his custom, he'd pulled out his work even before the jet began to rumble down the runway. She had slipped out of her mules, folded her legs to her side, and buried herself in a book.

Several hours ago, she'd put down the book she'd been reading and began nodding off. He'd had Stan, the steward, rouse her enough to offer her the use of the bedroom at the back of the plane, but she'd politely turned him down. At Stan's gentle insistence, though, she'd finally allowed him to lower one of the big lounge chairs so that she could lie down, and she'd accepted a pillow and a blanket. Then, without any sign of self-consciousness that he was sitting where he could see her, she'd fallen asleep.

He'd turned back to his work, but every now and then his gaze had involuntarily wandered to her. Some time ago she'd turned on her side, facing him. The blanket stopped at her waist, but its line showed him the length of her legs and the curve of her hips. Her lips were slightly parted and her hands were folded beneath her cheek as if she were a child. Even in sleep, it was as if she was incapable of looking awkward or less than lovely.

She stirred and quickly he averted his gaze to his work.

"Where are we?" she asked, her low, husky

voice reflecting that she'd just come up out of a deep sleep.

He glanced at his watch. "We're about an hour or so out of New York."

She sat up and stretched, her hands reaching for the ceiling, her fingertips gracefully pointed. Then, once again without any sign of self-consciousness, she stood and stretched a second time, going up on her tiptoes. As she did, the fitted T-shirt that hugged her breasts pulled upward from the loose waistband of her jeans, giving him a tantalizing glimpse of her navel. Then she bent from the waist, wrapped her arms around her legs, and pressed her face against her knees. Her long hair tumbled over her head, baring the nape of her neck, and her T-shirt climbed up her spine to reveal a strip of smooth, pale skin.

Warmth curled and twisted in his loins. She flattened her hands on the floor, then straightened and her hair flew over her head to settle around her shoulders.

He cleared his throat and pressed a button. "Are you hungry?"

"I could eat a little something."

Stan appeared. "Yes, sir?"

Nathan nodded toward Dani.

With a casual flip of her disheveled hair over her shoulder, Dani graced Stan with a grateful smile. "A cup of tea would be great. I'll make it."

"That won't be necessary. I can have that ready for you in a minute. But may I also offer you something else? I have some lovely steaks on board that I could broil."

She shook her head. "Thank you anyway, but I don't care for red meat."

"We stocked up on some wonderful farm chicken while we were in Paris."

She pressed her hand over her midriff. "I don't want to be a problem, but I'd like something light—scrambled eggs, for instance."

Stan looked perplexed. "I'd be happy to prepare scrambled eggs for you if that's what you'd really prefer."

"That would be wonderful."

"And what would you like with those scrambled eggs?"

"Nothing, thank you."

"Then perhaps a pastry afterward? I have a nice selection of fresh brioches, *pains au chocolat*, and croissants. They warm beautifully."

"Mmmm. A *pain au chocolat*, please." She glanced at Nathan. "Will you be joining me?"

He'd had hours to watch her sleep, and now that she was awake, he decided to put away his work and take advantage of this last hour with her. "I'd be happy to. Except, Stan, I'll have coffee, steak, and eggs."

"Yes, sir."

Dani reached for a carpetbag she'd brought on board, spun on her toes, and made her way toward the back of the plane, her posture perfectly erect. He craned his neck to watch her until she passed through the doorway, then slid closed behind her the panel that divided the cabin into rooms. She had to be a dancer, he thought. Only a trained dancer could carry herself so beautifully, yet be so unself-conscious about her body.

Minutes later she returned, her face moist and fresh from a wash, her hair gleaming from a thorough brushing. She'd also changed her top to another impossibly small T-shirt that hugged her body even more than the last, this one a grayed navy color.

"Did you have a nice rest?" he asked, even though he knew the answer.

"Yes, thank you." She settled herself on a couch across from him as Stan arranged a place setting on a table in front of her. "I had a lovely nap. How about yourself? Did you get any rest?"

"I worked most of the time."

She tilted her head and leveled an interested gaze at him. "You don't look tired."

"I've never needed that much sleep."

"So when we land in New York, you'll go to work then?"

He nodded. "I have a meeting tonight."

She stared at him. "What do you do? I mean, besides being a Damaron."

He chuckled at the way she'd phrased her question. "I work mainly in the financial end of our organization."

"Ah, a banker."

"I suppose you could say that, though no one ever has before."

"Then you must be the chief financial officer."

He shook his head. "None of us has a title."

A smile played around her lips. "So we'll just say that you work mainly in the financial end of your organization."

His gaze went to her lips. "Good plan."

She sat back while Stan set a small silver pot of hot water on a table in front of her, along with a fine porcelain cup and saucer. She chose a tea bag from a leather box that contained many different types of teas while Stan served Nathan coffee.

When the steward left, she looked over at Nathan. "There's something I've been wondering about."

"What's that?"

"Why would you want to take *me* to the ball?"

"Why wouldn't I?"

"You don't give much away, do you?"

To him, his question had been an answer, but apparently it hadn't satisfied her. He searched his mind for something that would. "I've been busy and I really hadn't given much thought to the ball until this past week when I realized it was just a few days away."

"Uh-huh, and so when you realized that, why didn't you simply pick up the phone, call your favorite lady, and ask her to come with you?"

"Because I don't have a favorite lady."

"In between relationships, then?"

Her persistence amused him. "I'm usually too busy for relationships."

"Relationships *do* require time."

"Sounds as if you're speaking from experience."

She hesitated and he thought he caught a glimpse of sadness in her eyes, but then it was gone. "Yes."

"I didn't even think to ask if you were involved."

A wry smile lighted her face. "I noticed and decided that it would probably be out of character for you if you did."

"Did you?" he asked, appreciating the curve of her lips and the glints of new humor in her eyes. "So are you involved?"

"No."

"Good, then there'll be no complications—although I've always found that complications usually aren't that complicated."

"Especially if you're you, which brings me back to my original question as to why *me*. You—"

She broke off as Stan reappeared with her scrambled eggs, then disappeared again. She took a sip of her tea, then a bite of scrambled eggs. "You must have a little black book. Why didn't you simply flip through it? There must be ladies lining up to get a date with you."

He liked her. He liked her a lot. If the kiss on the quay hadn't been enough, he was learning she was a warm and forthright person.

It was more than enough for him to decide he

wanted to spend more time with her. And there was more.

But it was the *more* that left him confused.

Nebulous things that fascinated and drew him to her. Like the graceful, unconscious way she moved. Like the sweet, stunning way a smile lit up her face. Like the way her hair fell around her face and down her back.

In the end he doubted he could give her an answer that would satisfy her, because he didn't have an answer that completely satisfied himself. Except he knew there wasn't one other woman he could think of with whom he'd rather spend Saturday night. Nor could he imagine he'd be happier going alone as had been his original plan. He ran several answers through his head before he decided on one that might make sense to her.

"Which is often the problem."

She looked up from her plate. "Excuse me?"

"The ladies who line up to get a date with me, as you said. They can be a problem, because they all want something from me, and believe me, they've got strings all over them." He shrugged. "I'm solving that problem by taking you to the ball."

"O-kay," she said, her tone clearly indicating she was still puzzled.

"You see, by coming with me, you're merely paying off a debt to me, so there'll be no complications. You also come with credentials—your father's—so no one will think it strange that you're there with me."

"As they would, no doubt, if they knew how we met."

"Exactly," he said, enjoying himself. He waved a careless hand toward her. "You're presentable. You'll know how to conduct yourself, and I'll be left free to do what I'm there for, which is to get people to write big, fat checks for our charity."

"You're a real bottom-line kind of guy, aren't you?"

"Always."

"And goodness, all those compliments, they may just go straight to my head."

He had thrown some of his best material at her and she'd caught it and thrown it right back, just as he'd hoped. "I'm glad we see things so much alike. I was sure you'd understand. Obviously, if you came to the ball with me and did nothing but have a fun date, it wouldn't be paying off a debt to me."

She nodded, then after a moment, she shook her head. "I may still be a wee bit shy of completely understanding the whole scope of this date."

"It's very simple. As I originally said, your presence at the ball will solve a lot of problems for me."

"And of course a man like you has so many problems."

"Right," he said with a nod, glad to see that humor still shone in her eyes.

"And just what will I have to do to solve your problems?"

He shrugged. "Nothing too hard. I will only require you to perform a small service for me."

"Excuse me, but the only *service* I agreed upon was to be your date."

"Right, and in doing so, you will be . . . doing a job, so to speak."

She pondered that a moment. "So let me understand this. To pay off my debt to you, I must attend the ball with you, but while doing so, I should look upon it as a job and not as an opportunity to have fun?"

"Mmmm, I'm afraid you don't quite have it yet. I said if you had *nothing* but fun, it wouldn't constitute paying off your debt."

"I see." She nodded. "I must suffer *part* of the time. Okay. So what type of suffering would you prefer?"

"Not suffering, just a little bit of work."

"Oh, we're back to the job part. Okay, I'm game. You have dishes that will need to be washed? Floors that need to be scrubbed? What?"

"More like debutantes and their mamas to be blocked, along with the odd divorced socialite or two."

"Oh, *blocked.* I'm glad you told me. I had no idea a ball would require wearing pads and a helmet."

He was hard-pressed not to laugh. "A gown will be fine."

"Really? Are you sure?"

"I figure anyone who could throw herself at me

as you did must know how to *prevent* someone else from doing the same thing."

She took another bite of her scrambled eggs and munched thoughtfully. "You know, Nathan, before meeting you, I had no idea a grown man could be so helpless and unable to simply tell a woman to leave him alone."

"I wasn't able to do it with you, now, was I?"

"You have a point there. As I recall, your message to me was a totally different one."

"Yes," he agreed softly. "It was. In fact, I wasn't ready for you to go when you did."

"I know," she murmured, looking down at her plate.

A charged silence fell between them, then Stan entered again, this time to serve Nathan his steak and eggs and refresh his coffee. He waited until Stan left. "At any rate, after this is all over, you'll thank me for having given you something to do. These things can be terribly dull."

"I suppose if it's something you do all the time, but a charity ball can accomplish a great deal of good, so in the end it must be worthwhile."

"That's why we do this one."

"We? Your family is underwriting it?"

"That's right. We want to add a new children's wing to the hospital this year."

"Then it *will* be all worth it."

Yes, he thought, gazing at her. He didn't know where their date would lead, but nevertheless, he had the feeling that it was definitely going to be worth it. "By the way, I've arranged for a car to meet you at the airport and drive you home."

"Thank you. That's very thoughtful, but I can take a cab."

"As I said, there will be a car to take you home. I'm also going to need your address so that I can pick you up Saturday night."

"Of course. I'll write it down for you before we land. You take the A train and get off at 125th Street. It's a brownstone."

"Harlem?" His brows drew together. "What are you doing up there?"

"I live there and I teach there."

"Teach what?"

"Ballet."

He'd been right, he reflected. She was a dancer.

"I have a small studio on the ground floor and an apartment above it."

"Who do you teach?"

"Anyone who wants to learn or continue in their studies."

"Do you teach full-time?"

She nodded. I also do the occasional performance as long as it doesn't interfere with my students, like the *Nutcracker* at Christmas, for instance. Likewise, I choreograph various productions. I also have a small corps of advanced dancers who perform on occasion."

He had a feeling that anything she did would be enchanting. "I'd like to see you perform."

"You will." She smiled at him. "Saturday night. Isn't that going to be my job? To perform as a blocker?"

"No." Sitting cross-legged on her sister's bed, Dani shook her head at the bright green spangled evening gown Natalie was holding up for her approval.

"Okay." Natalie tossed it onto a growing pile of gowns on her chaise longue, returned to her closet, and several moments later reappeared with a long black sheath. "How about this one?"

"No. I have no breasts. There's no way I could hold that one up."

"A seamstress can give it a tuck here and there, and it would be perfect."

Dani shook her head. "No, it's you, not me."

"That must be why it's in my closet and not yours," Natalie mumbled. She cast a rueful gaze at the heap of gowns Dani had already refused, then sighed. "Don't worry, sweetie. It's not for nothing that I'm married to a man who loves going out to any and every event in town. In fact, the Damaron party list must be about the only one we're not on."

"Sorry I can't help you. This is a onetime shot for me."

Natalie chuckled. "Somehow I think I'll manage to get along without yet another charity event to attend. Who knows? Maybe I'll even have a romantic evening with my husband. Stranger things have happened. But back to your problem. I've still got half a closetful here you haven't seen."

"You own a lot of fabulous gowns, Nat, but let's face it, you and I are totally different when it comes to the way we dress. You're designer clothes. I'm more . . . thrift shops."

"Nonsense. With your graceful body, you can wear anything."

In a pinch, she and her sister could wear each other's clothes. Basically they'd always had the same body type, but in the process of giving birth to two beautiful children, Natalie's body had filled out more. "In fact, I probably don't have a style."

"You dress like *you*, which is flat-out beautiful, even when you're wearing jeans or leotards." Hopefully, she held up a sophisticated pleated column of white. "How about this one?"

Dani shook her head at the gown. "You know what? I think one of my problems is that I just can't get over the fact that Nathan sent me a gown to wear." She thumped the large box she'd brought with her so that she could show its contents to her sister.

Natalie tossed the latest gown aside and sat down beside Dani on the end of the bed. "I'm sure his intentions were good."

"I suppose."

"Oh, come on. You told him what you do. You told him you pay your own way. It wouldn't take a brain surgeon to figure out you don't have closets and closets of clothes. I'm sure he didn't want to put you in an embarrassing situation."

"You're probably right. It's just the idea that really gets me. I'm going to send it back."

"Are you sure you should? I mean, you haven't found anything else to wear yet. Let me see it again."

Dani lifted the top of the box. Inside was a black lace sheath with long sleeves and a scooped neckline. The entire bodice of the dress glittered with black beads and paillettes.

"It's magnificent," Natalie said as she pulled it out of the box. "It's your size, honey, plus, this black would look stunning on you."

"Those beads weigh twenty pounds if they weigh an ounce. I wouldn't be able to move. Who in the world do you think picked this out anyway?"

"Probably a personal shopper, who, by the way, has excellent taste. This is a designer original."

"Of course it is," Dani said gloomily. She pushed at the heavy bodice. "You know, the real problem is that I said yes to this whole thing at all."

"Nuh-uh. The real problem would have been if you'd said *no*, because then I would have really worried about you." Her sister's gaze softened on her. "You know, Dani, you haven't gone out with any man since Gil."

"I know," she said, taking the dress from her sister and staring down at it.

"That was nine years ago. It's about time you

got out, don't you think? I mean, with someone other than that group of friends you run around with."

"There hasn't been anyone I felt was worth the effort of an actual date."

"Until now, you mean."

Dani looked at her sister. "Until now."

THREE

"Didn't you like the dress I had sent to you?"

The rumble of Nathan's deep voice skittered along Dani's nerve endings. It was the first remark he'd made about the dress he'd sent her. She looked over at him.

He was sitting next to her at the large, round table he had been assigned to host. Each of his cousins had also been given his or her own table. Now the dinner portion of the evening was drawing to a close, and people were already beginning to split up into different groups while others milled about.

Surprisingly, Nathan had kept her by his side up to now. Even though he had been responsible for making sure that everyone at their table had had an interesting and relaxed dinner hour, he'd also somehow managed to make her feel as if she were the most important person in the room and that he was aware of every breath she drew. An interesting talent. A very seductive talent. "The dress was lovely, but I'm perfectly capable of outfitting myself."

He turned his upper body toward her so that the person on his other side would be shut out of their conversation, while the intimacy of his expression and the low timbre of his voice kept the person on her other side from joining in. "I didn't say you weren't. The dress was my way of—"

"Ensuring that I wouldn't embarrass you by not having anything appropriate to wear," she said, her voice equally low as she finished his sentence.

He grinned wryly. "Believe it or not, I wasn't thinking of myself. I didn't want *you* to be embarrassed."

She chuckled. "Do I honestly seem like the type of woman who wouldn't know what would and wouldn't be correct to wear to a function such as this one?"

"No, but—"

"And if I didn't own such a garment, do I seem like the type of woman who wouldn't be resourceful enough to come up with something to wear anyway?"

"No, but—"

Deciding to let him off the hook, she smiled. "Don't worry about it, Nathan. It was very kind of you to even think of the gown. Really. I'm surprised you even gave the matter a thought."

He slid his arm around the back of her chair and

leaned closer to her. "Do I seem like the kind of man who would be incapable of being kind?"

"Touché. Sending me the gown was definitely a kind act and I thank you for it."

"Even though you sent it back?"

"I knew I'd feel more comfortable if I was wearing something of my own. It's just a personal quirk of mine, but I need to feel as if I can really move in the things I wear. And as utterly wonderful as the gown you sent was, it would have weighed me down."

He tilted his head and studied her, as if he found her remarks odd. The warmth of his body was so strong, she could feel it on her skin. His scent of dark spices and potent sexuality filled the air between them. By default she was forced to breathe him in. Not that it was any hardship.

"The dress had about twenty pounds of beads on it," she said in further explanation.

"I'm sorry," he finally said, and funny enough she knew he meant it. "I'm afraid I didn't have time to go out and choose the dress myself, and all my assistant told me about it was that it was black."

"Don't apologize." Her reaction to his sincerity softened her voice. "As I said, it was a very kind thing for you to do, but it just wasn't necessary."

In the end she'd gone home empty-handed from her sister's and delved into her own closet. The dress she'd ultimately decided to wear was very simple, very light. There was a silk strapless underdress of mist blue, then a one-shouldered overdress made out of sheer silk chiffon in the water colors of mauves, greens, and blues. A graceful, floating dress, its skirt fell to an asymmetrical hem, on one side cascading downward in uneven gossamer layers to her feet, the other side stopping at her knees. A handful of blue sequins resembling glistening drops of water were randomly scattered over the dress. A pair of high-heeled silver sandals and a silver slide to hold her long hair back completed the ensemble.

His gaze dropped to scan the bodice, then returned to her face. "You look beautiful and your dress is exquisite. In fact, there's no one here who can touch the way you look tonight."

Warmth flooded up beneath her skin to her face. "That's quite a compliment, considering your three female cousins are here, plus quite a few Damaron wives." She'd already met most of them and had liked them very much.

"I wouldn't say it unless it was true."

The thing was, she believed him, and she was all the more flustered that she did. Restless beneath his scrutiny, she absently fingered the skirt of the dress. It was so familiar to her. The fabric, its fit, the graceful way it hung on her, the happy memories it held—it was like wearing the comfort of an old friend, which she supposed was ultimately why she chose it.

"Besides," he continued, "ninety percent of the women here tonight are wearing black. The ball is in imminent danger of resembling a convocation of crows—with you as the only bluebird," he finished softly.

"Water sprite, actually."

"I beg your pardon?"

"This was my costume when I danced the role of Ondine."

"You as a water sprite?" He stared at her for a moment. "Yes," he said slowly. "There is a poetry about you."

"Thank you," she murmured, again unprepared for the honesty of his compliment. "Actually, I would normally wear the dress over a leotard, but for the ball, I decided to make an underdress instead."

"You *made* it?"

She laughed again, this time at his surprise. "I love to sew. And most of the time it's cheaper to make the costumes my students wear in our productions."

A man she'd met when they first arrived came up and whispered something in Nathan's ear. She'd met so many people already that evening that she couldn't remember his name, but he'd been doing the same thing on and off all evening. Mentally she'd pegged him as Nathan's aide-de-camp. The man slipped away and Nathan looked back at her. "I'm afraid I'm going to have to go to work in a minute. Come with me. I have to make a little speech, but that won't take long. Afterward I'll be forced to mingle and I'm not very good at it."

She smiled. "I don't believe that for a minute.

Besides, I was thinking of going to the ladies' room. Do you know where it is?" Even though she was enjoying herself immensely, she was more than ready for a break from him. The full strength of his attention required her to be on her toes at all times.

When her gaze followed the direction where he pointed, she saw an older woman sitting at a table, seemingly isolated, though every seat at the table was occupied. "Who is that lady? She's been watching me off and on tonight." Unlike the other women at her table, the woman in question was wearing lavender, a color that didn't suit her at all.

"That's Helene Sorge. She's the widow of the steel magnate Horace Sorge."

The name meant nothing to her, but she didn't have to be told to know that Helene Sorge was a formidable woman. Her posture was excruciatingly correct, her demeanor stiff, and there was something about her that plainly said she didn't suffer fools gladly. "She looks lonely."

He grinned and her attention was drawn back to him. Involuntarily her gaze fastened on his lips and the memory of the way they had kissed on the quay several nights before came rushing back to her. Warmth stirred in her and she wondered if tonight he would kiss her again. And if so, would it be as wonderful as that first kiss had been?

"That's certainly an interesting take on Helene," he said. "The two women on either side of her are her best friends."

"But they're ignoring her."

"It's more like she's ignoring them. She doesn't encourage familiarity. She's always been that way, but it's gotten worse the last year. A little over a year ago her daughter and son-in-law were killed in a car accident and her granddaughter was severely hurt."

"How awful. Maybe that's why she looks as if she's closed in on herself."

"You have a very unique way of seeing people. However, in my experience, Helene Sorge is simply a very hard woman to get along with. I've seen her snap the head off a person simply because the person dared to try to talk to her. She comes to things like this because she sees it as her duty to carry on the charity endeavors that her husband considered important when he was alive. But at the same time she lets it be known she hates being at events like this. God forbid she should enjoy herself."

"That's a shame," she murmured, trying to concentrate on what he was saying, rather than on the question of whether or not he would kiss her before the night was over. "Life is too short for a person to be that unhappy."

"I agree. And she's enormously wealthy, but she's cheap, just as her husband was. Horace died twelve years ago, yet she still continues to write checks for the measly amount he was giving when he died, with no thought to inflation. When one of us tries to contact her about it, she always cuts us off." He shrugged. "We've found it easier to give her a wide berth."

"Why do you think she's been staring at me?"

"I'm not sure except what I said before." His eyes softened on her. "You're the most beautiful woman here tonight."

His compliments were overwhelming. His low, husky voice was playing her nerves as if they were an instrument. His intimately possessive body language had her melting inside. Suddenly he leaned forward and pressed a kiss to her cheek. "I've got to go. When you get back from the ladies' room, come find me."

She couldn't help but smile. "So I can continue blocking all those debutantes and socialites who are constantly throwing themselves at you?"

She'd seen a few women send longing glances his way. In fact, she'd been embarrassed for them because of the naked emotion in their expressions. There was no doubt about it—Nathan was definitely a man who inspired passion of all kinds in women. So far, though, no one had had to be peeled off him. It was something she sincerely regretted, since she was planning to leave him to his own devices for the kick of seeing how he got himself out of it.

He smiled wryly. "The women take one look at you and give up. I knew you'd be great at blocking them."

She laughed, deciding not to believe all his compliments. It was easier on her that way, because he was getting to her. In subtle, indefinable ways, he was definitely getting to her.

———◆————————————◆———

Dani lingered in the lounge area of the ladies' room, pretending to check her makeup and correct a nonexistent flaw in her mascara. But in reality, she was giving herself a respite from the high energy of the crowd. She engaged in idle conversation with several women and quite a few stopped to compliment her on her dress.

Some of their compliments were sincere. Some weren't. But without exception, the underlying thread in all their conversations had been curiosity about her. Obviously the word had gotten around that Nathan Damaron had brought someone new to the ball.

She could see how it might be disconcerting to them. Since they didn't know her, or how she and Nathan had met, or even how long they'd known each other, they couldn't satisfactorily slot her into a category, such as serious contender or casual fling. And she didn't help them. Instead, she chose to keep her own counsel and to simply say thank you for the compliments.

Because she didn't know any of them, she couldn't say for certain whether or not she would have anything in common with them, but she led a very low-key life. Chances were excellent she would never see them again.

When she returned to the ballroom, she saw the Damaron family on the stage, taking turns speaking about their hopes and plans for the new children's wing for the hospital. Since they were behind the project, she had no doubt the wing would become a reality. Listening to them and hearing their dedication to bringing this new state-of-the-art facility into being made her happy that she'd come. The hospital was a cause she could get behind—not actively—but she did plan to write a small check and send it in.

As she stood in the back, listening, her eyes wandered the crowd, and once again the older woman caught her attention. Helene Sorge's gaze was on the stage, but Dani had the feeling the woman wasn't really hearing anything.

Nathan had said that giving the woman a wide berth was best, but during the evening her gaze had gone back to her more than once. For one thing, she'd caught Helene staring at her every now and then. But the real reason she found the woman compelling was that she saw loneliness in her when apparently others around her saw only a rude, self-sufficient woman.

The chair beside Helene was empty, and on impulse she went over and sat down. "Good evening, Mrs. Sorge," she said softly. "I'm Danielle Savourat."

At the sound of her voice, the woman started, then turned toward her and pinned her with an icy gaze. "I beg your pardon?"

"I'm Danielle Savourat, and Nathan Damaron told me you are Helene Sorge."

The woman's brows shot up. "Did I inadvertently do something that in any way led you to believe I would welcome your company?"

"No, but—"

"Good. Then please leave me alone." She had a foghornlike voice that she made no attempt to soften.

"Mrs. Sorge, I saw you staring at me several times this evening and was wondering why."

Her eyes narrowed on her. "I *told* you to leave me alone. Exactly what word didn't you understand?"

Her loud voice carried and more than one person turned around to see who had been stupid enough to awaken the sleeping bear. "I understood all of the words—thank you for asking. I simply thought you looked alone and I—"

The angry look the woman gave her startled and silenced Dani. Rudeness was one thing, she reflected, but why would the woman be angry that someone had taken the time to speak with her? She supposed Helene Sorge was accustomed to people doing exactly as she said and that no doubt would include not approaching her without her permission.

Helene Sorge's cold-eyed gaze quickly ran over her. "And *what* in the world are you wearing? It looks like a ballet costume for *Ondine*."

She was the first person tonight to know what her dress was. Dani ventured a tentative smile. "That's because it is."

"Why on *earth* would you wear a ballet costume to a charity ball?"

"Because it was all I could find to wear that was comfortable."

"*Comfortable.*" She harrumphed. "Whatever gave you the idea that you were supposed to be comfortable at one of these things?"

"I'm afraid I didn't know there was some sort of dress code about discomfort. I've always believed it was more important to be comfortable, especially when one is going to be in a situation where emotionally one might not be particularly at ease. Beyond that, why should you spend one minute of your life in discomfort if you don't have to?"

"What an odd little thing you are." Helene paused. "So you're a ballerina."

"I used to be, but I was injured, and now I'm a ballet teacher."

Interest flitted in and out of the older woman's expression. "How badly were you injured?"

She hadn't been prepared for Helene to actually show interest in her. She'd merely seen a lonely woman who, in her opinion, needed a little distraction from unhappy thoughts. She'd simply decided to see if she could get her to talk. Now that Helene had, Dani had no one to blame but herself. Once again, her impulses had engaged before her brain.

"I had quite a few broken bones, along with several other serious problems. Both of my legs were broken. They healed well, but slowly. Still, with a more extensive and rigorous program of physical therapy, I'm convinced I could have returned to the dance full-time. In the end, however, I decided not to."

"Why not?" The question came out as an attack. "Wasn't your dedication strong enough?"

"My dedication was never in question. Ballet has always been my life, but the accident . . . that is, the injuries changed me in a lot of ways. It made me see life differently and I realized I wasn't sure what I wanted to do with the rest of my life."

"What did you finally decide?" Helene asked, her voice no longer like a foghorn at full volume.

"I decided to teach ballet to all those who wanted to learn, regardless of their age, financial status, body type, or talent."

"How odd."

Dani chuckled. "Maybe. But to be a successful dancer one must focus all one's energies into one-self. To be a successful teacher, one must focus all one's energies outward to help others. That's what I decided I wanted to do, and I love it."

Helene looked away from her, and since the Damarons were no longer on the stage, Dani took the opportunity to see if she could pick out Nathan from among the now mingling crowd. She couldn't. The orchestra had started to play again and through the crowd, she could see that a few couples had started to dance.

"Call me Helene."

Dani's head jerked around in surprise. "Thank you, Helene. And please call me Dani."

"Dani?" She frowned. "I will call you Danielle."

Dani smothered a smile. "Very well."

"Danielle, did that Damaron you're with to-night tell you that I lost my daughter in an automobile accident?"

"Yes, he did, and by the way, his name is Nathan. He also said your son-in-law was killed, too, and that your granddaughter was severely injured."

"Did he tell you that he pitied me?"

"No, he didn't."

She looked away. "I hate pity."

"There's nothing wrong with pity if it's well-meant. Really, it's just another form of sympathy." She took a moment to organize her thoughts. "You know, when you lose someone you love very much, people are often at a loss to know what to say or how to help. Maybe they say or do the wrong thing, but they're well-intentioned and they shouldn't be faulted for trying. The truth is, there's really not much anyone can say or do to help you get over the pain of losing someone you loved."

Helene's eyes were moist when she looked back at Dani. "You really are the most peculiar girl." She paused. "It sounds as if you've experienced what you're talking about."

"I have."

Helene fell silent, and Dani took the opportunity to scan the crowd once again. She found Nathan talking with someone who she couldn't see. But then Yasmine walked up to him. Yasmine was one of his cousins and Dani remembered her name because she was so extraordinary-looking, all golden and beautiful. But her effect on Nathan was even more extraordinary. As soon as he saw her, his demeanor immediately changed. He threw a casual arm around her, drew her to his side, pressed a kiss to her forehead, then smiled lovingly down at her.

Something about his actions moved Dani in a way she couldn't define. Thinking about it, she supposed it was the first time she'd seen Nathan exhibit genuine warmth.

After the kiss at the hotel in Paris, he had treated her more as an adversary. Tonight he was treating her as a desirable woman. There was no doubt he was giving her the full-court press of his charms, because he wanted something. *Her.* She knew it, understood it, and somewhat to her surprise, she liked and welcomed it.

But with Yasmine, he'd reacted naturally rather than for effect. He hadn't known if anyone was watching him and he obviously hadn't cared. At that moment when he'd drawn Yasmine into his arms, he hadn't been concerned with image or what other people thought. He didn't want anything from Yasmine and she didn't want anything from him. They were completely at ease with one another and the love he'd showed her had been real, simple, and pure. What would it be like, she wondered, to be the recipient of such casual, uncensored warmth and love from him?

"You remind me of my daughter in several ways."

She looked back at Helene. "Really?"

"Your coloring. The way you move. My daughter loved the ballet and studied it for a great number of years. I had hopes that my granddaughter would follow in her mother's steps, but since the accident . . ." Her voice trailed off and she wearily shook her head.

"What is your granddaughter's name?"

"Cecilia."

"And how is she doing?"

"Her injuries have left her with several problems—joint stiffness, a limp, a couple of other minor things. I believe a large part of her problem is psychological. She used to be such a happy girl, but now . . . I've brought in the finest specialists to see her. They tell me she won't get any better unless she tries, but she's closed herself off from everyone and I don't know how to talk to her."

"Since that's what you've done yourself?"

Sharp eyes cut to her. "You're not only odd and peculiar, you're extremely impertinent."

"Maybe, but I think I could help your granddaughter. At least I'd like to try."

"That's *out* of the question. You're not a doctor!"

"I never claimed to be." She stared at the older woman, rigid in her pain. "What do you have to lose, Helene? If I *can't* help her, the worst thing that would happen is that your granddaughter would be exposed to someone new with perhaps a new way of thinking."

Helene scowled coldly at her. "It wouldn't work."

"Dani?" She lifted her head to see Nathan bent over her. "Is everything all right?"

She smiled up at him. "Everything's fine. You know Helene Sorge, of course."

"Yes." He leaned over and offered his hand.

After a noticeable hesitation Helene took it. "Which one are you?"

Dani hid a smile. Helene knew his name because she'd told her, but then she had the feeling she'd known all along. It was just her way to put everyone on the defensive.

"I'm Nathan."

"Well, Nathan, your new hospital wing sounds like a fine idea. You can count on my usual amount."

Nathan's pleasant expression never once changed. "We appreciate that. Thank you."

The impulse came from nowhere, and before Dani could stop herself, the words were slipping out of her mouth. "Helene, give me a chance to see if I can help your granddaughter. I'll come to her the first time. If we hit it off, and if it looks as if I can help her, you promise Nathan that you'll double the amount you normally give."

She heard Nathan make a choking sound and Helene seemed stunned into silence. Dani looked from one to the other. "Why not? I think it's a great idea."

"Dani," Nathan started, and reached for her

arm to pull her up. "I think it's probably best if we don't impose on—"

"What's the matter with you, Damaron? Don't you have any confidence in this little thing you brought this evening?"

"Uh, of course I do."

Helene looked at her. "You can't possibly help her, and if you try, you're doomed to fail. You haven't even met her. You don't even know about all her physical problems, much less her psychological problems."

"You're right. I don't. How old is Cecilia?"

"She's ten."

Dani nodded. "Helene, I've been through quite a bit of what she's going through. That alone should help, if I can just get her to listen to me. Plus, I've helped other children with other types of problems. So maybe I can help her, maybe I can't. But in any event, I see no harm in trying. If I do help her, her life will be changed. She'll become a happy child again. With that possibility, how can you not allow me to try?"

"I suppose I have to, don't I?" Helene conceded ungraciously.

Dani smiled. "You won't be sorry." She looked up at Nathan. "And you may get double your usual contribution for your hospital wing."

Helene's mouth tightened. "In the exceedingly unlikely event you can help my granddaughter, I'll quadruple the amount."

Nathan sounded as if he was choking again, but

Dani laughed. "That's wonderful. Isn't it, Nathan?" She glanced at him and immediately had another idea. "Helene, I wonder if . . ." She cleared her throat. "Have you already written the check you planned to give the Damarons tonight?"

"Of course I have. It's in my purse." She pulled it out of her purple satin evening bag and handed it to Nathan.

"Thank you, Helene. As always, your contribution is greatly appreciated."

Helene nodded, then before she could close her bag, Dani put her hand over hers. "As a personal favor to me, would you mind giving Nathan a dollar more?"

"Whatever for?"

"As I said, as a favor for me."

Helene looked up at Nathan. "This is a very peculiar girl."

"I know," he said, his expression and tone clearly indicating he thought Dani had lost her mind.

Helene pulled a dollar bill out of her purse and handed it over to him, then she looked at Dani. "Shall we say ten sharp tomorrow morning? Damaron knows where I live."

"I'm sorry, but I can't make it tomorrow. I have a prior commitment."

"Dani, I'm sure your commitment can be changed," Nathan said.

"No, it can't. But I can make Monday afternoon, around two."

Helene scowled. "That's as soon as you can make it?"

"I'm afraid so."

"Well, then," Helene said, her posture taut with displeasure, "I guess I'll see you then."

FOUR

"Whatever possessed you?" Nathan murmured into her ear as he danced her around the floor.

"Possessed me?" Dani felt as if she were floating. Nathan had hurried her away from Helene and drawn her onto the dance floor and into his arms. A dancer for most of her life, she could dance with just about anyone, no matter how awkward they were.

But in Nathan she'd found an extraordinary partner. With his strong arms around her, she didn't even have to think about what she was doing. It was like a perfect *pas de deux* where her partner knew her steps as well as his own. She could relax and enjoy the sensations of being held close against his body and allow him to lead her.

"Whatever possessed you to approach Helene Sorge?"

"I thought she looked lonely. I told you that before you left the table."

"Yes, but I assumed after I'd explained how formidable and unpleasant a woman she was, you'd know not to go anywhere near her."

She pulled her head back and looked up at him with a grin. "Who are you worried about? Me or her? Are you afraid I offended her?"

"No one can talk with Helene for any length of time without offending her," he said dryly, "so no, I'm not concerned about her. I'm concerned about you."

"Well, you needn't be."

"Okay, so how did you even get Helene to talk with you?"

"I just went over to her and introduced myself."

"And she didn't cut you dead?"

"She tried, but I persevered."

"But why?" he asked, never missing a step.

"Because I wanted to." His perplexed frown told her she hadn't given him an answer that had satisfied him. "It was another one of my impulses and I went with it because she looked as if she needed someone to talk to."

"Another one of your impulses? You mean like the one when you saw me and decided I looked as if I needed someone to kiss me?"

Her heart skipped a beat as it did every time she thought about the kiss. In this case she also chuckled. "I didn't decide you needed someone to kiss you. I decided *I* wouldn't mind kissing you."

"As it turned out, I didn't mind kissing you either. And we need to kiss each other again very soon. And that will be just for starters."

Her heart thudded, then took up a rapid beat. "You've, um, gotten off the subject."

"Guilty. But you need to know that very soon now, kissing you and making love to you are going to be the *only* subjects we talk about. *If* we talk at all."

Heat burned in his eyes and on her skin where he touched her. And deeper inside her, an aching need filled her. The anticipation of what would come had her aroused to the point that she wanted Nathan to start kissing her right there and then and not stop until they were both sated. But she knew he couldn't. This was an event to raise money for a tremendously good cause, and people needed to be focused on giving money, not on two people in heat on the dance floor. "So, uh, getting back to Helene?"

"Right," he said, his voice rough. Then he let out a long breath, making her realize that he'd been thinking the same thing as she. "I've known Helene Sorge much longer than you and I've never once sensed she needed someone to talk to." He paused, his gaze briefly lowering to her lips. The dance floor was crowded, but in moments like this it seemed to her they were the only two people there. "So why were you the only one in the place that received that impression?"

"Maybe because I'm the only one in the place who took time to really look at her.

He shook his head wryly. "You really are incredible and I have to thank you. I can't believe she said she'd quadruple her donation."

"Don't spend it yet. Quadrupling the money is dependent on whether or not I can help her granddaughter."

"You already accomplished a miracle simply by getting her to come out with that statement. I have no doubt you can perform another one."

She laughed. "Thank you for your confidence, but Cecilia sounds like a little girl with a lot of problems."

"And you still think you can help her?"

"I hope so."

"Hope?" He groaned good-naturedly. "Don't tell me, let me guess. It was an impulse that made you offer to help the girl."

"Maybe," she said a bit defensively. "But I really do want to help her."

"I think that's wonderful."

His tone had turned tender and it rasped along her skin, bringing up warmth as it went. He was looking down at her as if he were going to devour her. Everything about him said he wanted her, and heaven help her, she wanted him too. When had she turned into this carnal person?

The thing was, she didn't know if she'd ever see him after tonight. One of the reasons he'd said he'd invited her was that she came with no strings. But a little while ago, she'd had another impulse.

She conjured up a playful smile. "I hope you still think that after you realize what's really happened."

"What do you mean?"

"Remember that extra dollar I asked Helene to give you?"

He nodded. "I meant to ask you about that. What was that about?"

It had been about providing her with the opportunity to see him again, but it would all depend on whether he wanted to continue their game. She hoped he would. She also hoped that somewhere down the line she didn't have reason to regret all her impulses. "You said that for the last twelve years Helene's given you the same miserly amount."

"That's right."

"But tonight I got her to give you a dollar over that amount."

"Right again."

He didn't have a clue what was coming, she reflected with delight. "Which means *you* now owe *me*."

"I now . . . ? *Damn*." He gave another good-natured groan. "I can't believe you got me like that."

She laughed. "Sorry, but you made me pay up when you said I owed you. Now turnabout is fair play."

Humor glinted in his dark eyes. "I think I'll hold off on deciding whether or not it's fair play.

What are you going to make me do? Clean your house with a toothbrush?"

"That's not a bad idea at all, but I have something in mind that may be harder for you to do than that."

"I just bet you do," he drawled.

Heat curled in her stomach and made its way down to her toes at the appreciation in his gaze and tone. "How do you feel about kids?"

"It depends. Whose kids?"

"My kids—in a manner of speaking, that is. Kids that are my ballet students."

"You want me to sign up for one of your ballet classes?"

She laughed. "Gee, I wish I'd thought of that."

"No way."

"Okay, then, do you have a sport utility vehicle or a van of some sort you could use tomorrow afternoon?"

"Yes." His answer was wary. "Are you moving? Do you want me to help you pack and move? Because if so, I'd rather pay for movers."

She grinned. "Boy, are you suspicious."

"I find I'm rarely wrong to be."

"Well, this time you are."

He smiled ruefully. "Okay, Dani. No more guesses. Lay it on me."

They were barely dancing now. Instead they were simply swaying to the beat, an excuse to keep their bodies pressed together. "It's much like the job you gave me. A little fun, a little work." She saw a gleam of humor in the dark depths of his eyes. Encouraged, she went on. "Each spring, it's a tradition of mine to have a wiener roast in the park for my students."

"Wiener roast?"

She giggled. "You say that as if it's something foreign."

"I was just trying to recall if I've ever been on one."

"And?"

"And I've never been to an actual wiener roast where nothing other than hot dogs was served."

"Well, that's all you'll get tomorrow since that's all my budget will run to this year. I spent the rest of my money on a little surprise for my students."

"Wait a minute. Don't dismiss me completely in the wiener-roast category yet." She watched the frown crease his forehead as he thought back in his past. "Before my parents were killed, we used to have cookouts, with hamburgers, hot dogs, potato salad, baked beans, potato chips, that sort of thing. Does that qualify?"

"You bet."

"Good."

Dani hid a smile at Nathan's competitiveness. It was such a little thing, but he couldn't stand even the idea of being unable to say he'd been involved in a wiener roast.

"Okay," he went on. "So you haven't told me yet where *my* part in this comes in."

His part was to spend more time with her, she

reflected, so that she could figure out not only why she wanted to be with him so much, but how that need might affect her life. "You get to come and help me."

"Do I?" He chuckled.

"Sure, and anyway—what greater way to spend your Sunday afternoon?"

"Oh, is this the prior commitment you told Helene about?"

"That's right. There was no way I would call it off. It's something my kids look forward to every year."

"Who usually helps you?"

She shrugged one shoulder. "Sometimes friends, sometimes parents, especially if they happen to have a sport utility or a van. Everyone meets at my studio around eleven-thirty in the morning. Once at the park, we play games, eat, and generally have an all-around great time."

"You mentioned eating?"

She grinned. "Oh, trust me, you won't starve. Around one, I fire up the grill and everyone comes running."

"Sounds like a lot of fun," he said in a tone that clearly implied otherwise.

She laughed, aware of the surreptitious glances coming their way from other dancers, but she couldn't tear her gaze away from him. "I knew you'd like the idea."

"Interesting that you'd think that," he said dryly. "How long will it last?"

"Until the last kid goes home."

"Great," he said gloomily, but the twinkle in his eyes said he was teasing her. "I've never known a kid who would willingly go home from a park."

"Don't worry. They eventually wear themselves out."

His gaze softened as he looked down at her. "Then I guess you've got me."

"Wonderful." And now that she had him, she mused, what would she do with him?

"Excuse me, Nathan, Dani."

Dani looked around. "Hi, Lion."

He smiled at her. "Having a good time?"

Grinning, she looked back at Nathan. "I'm having a very entertaining time."

Nathan studied his cousin. "What's up?"

"May I speak with you privately?"

She felt Nathan's body tense against hers. "Certainly. Dani?" Taking her hand, he led her off the dance floor and back to their table. He waited while she settled herself in a chair, then bent and murmured, "I'll be right back."

He stepped off to one side with Lion and listened as his cousin spoke quietly with him. As Dani watched, Nathan's expression became more and more grim.

Finally, with a nod at Lion, he turned back toward her and knelt in front of her. "I'm sorry, Dani, but I'm going to have to leave you for an emergency meeting and I don't know how long it will run."

"Is something wrong?"

"I'm afraid so. One of our cousins has a problem and needs help."

"Someone here tonight?"

He shook his head. "In South America." He stood, took her hand again, and pulled her to her feet. "I'm really sorry, but I'm going to have to end our evening."

"Don't apologize. Besides"—she smiled—"my job is done anyway."

He looked blank for a moment. "Job? Oh, right. Your job." A brief smiled touched his lips. "You did great, by the way. Thank you."

"You're welcome. I have to say it was tough, but I managed to persevere and keep all those women away from you." He chuckled, but she could tell his mind was already elsewhere. "Go on. I can see that you're worried."

He nodded. "My driver will take you home tonight and I'll see you tomorrow."

"Your driver doesn't need to take me home. You may need him."

"My driver will take you home," he repeated, then pressed a firm kiss to her lips.

The kiss didn't last very long, but the mere touch of his lips on hers left a lingering burn.

An hour later, at home in bed, Dani admitted to herself that she was disappointed they'd had to cut their evening so short. Dancing in his arms had been a memorable, sensual experience that she couldn't forget. Her dress had been so thin, it had seemed to her she could feel each muscle in his body as he moved them both over the floor. And despite the sexual tension between them, she'd felt strangely comfortable in his arms, so comfortable she'd let him lead her. Amazing when she thought about it, but then Nathan was turning out to be the most amazing man she'd ever met.

Dani watched as three of her ballet students, two little girls and one boy, shrieking with laughter, piled on top of Nathan, pushing him back onto the grass. He pulled them with him, so that soon they were all four sprawled on the grass, laughing.

She'd been relieved when Nathan had shown up this morning at her studio at the appointed time, his worried expression of the night before gone. He'd told her that they'd been able to get his cousin out of whatever situation he'd been in and that he was now safe. Then he'd kissed her hello with such ease and sense of entitlement, an onlooker might have thought they'd been seeing each other a year instead of the matter of days it had been.

After the kiss he had rolled up his sleeves and, without complaint or excuse, had gone to work doing whatever she'd needed. His competence in handling all parts of a children's picnic hadn't surprised her. What had, however, was how easily he'd joined in the fun.

The kids had taken to him immediately. He'd kicked off his shoes and joined them in toe painting, her version of finger painting. And he'd refereed the potato-sack roll, two kids in the same potato sack, rolling toward the finish line, her version of the three-legged race. In short, he'd been marvelous all afternoon.

He'd merely blinked when the horse she'd hired arrived with its owner. It had taken her months to find just the right horse and ask favors from friends and friends of friends to obtain the proper clearances. Then she'd secretly had to get the permission slips signed by the parents. But in the end it turned out to be all worth it. When the kids saw the horse, they'd gone crazy.

As soon as Nathan had gotten over the shock of realizing she'd actually rented a horse to be part of their cookout, he stepped forward and began to organize the kids in the order in which they'd ride.

Plainly he was a natural with children. Right now he was holding one of the youngest of her students, five-year-old Mary Anne, in his lap, and she realized something she hadn't thought of before. Nathan was the kind of man to whom family was all-important. He would definitely want a family of his own. The knowledge hit her hard.

Deliberately she turned her back on the scene and began to tidy up, putting away the leftovers and throwing away their trash.

From the time she'd first kissed him until now, impulse had driven her in the things she'd said to him and done with him. So far he'd made her feel things she never could have imagined. If it went much further with him, she knew she'd be in way over her head.

The thing was, she wanted it to go further.

For nine years she'd barely given any man a second glance unless he'd been a friend. Her grieving for Gil had been fierce. Compounding her grief had been the fact that she'd also lost the baby she had been unknowingly carrying at the time. During the days following the accident, her emotional pain had seemed unbearable.

But life had continued around her and eventually she'd made a decision. She'd learned that there was a place deep inside her that would always mourn the losses she'd suffered on that long-ago night when she and Gil had ridden out to the countryside on his motorcycle and he'd taken a corner too fast and lost control. But she'd also learned that it was time to go on. And she had. With her dancing and teaching, she'd been fulfilled and satisfied, but there'd been no new love for her, no deep, soul-baring connection with another man.

And then she'd met Nathan. She'd kissed him. And quite suddenly she'd felt the stirrings of desire for him. He was the first man since the accident who had made her want more than a friendship, more than a mere surface connection. And to be honest with herself, it wouldn't be possible for her to simply be a friend of Nathan's. At this stage she was just beginning to realize that with him she might want it all. Unfortunately, she now knew it wasn't going to happen.

Guillermo Santos had been in her first ballet class. He'd been her friend, then her partner, and then her lover. They'd shared a deep, simple, and comfortable love.

But with Nathan, there was nothing uncomplicated or comfortable about the way he made her feel. With him, she felt like a cat on a hot tin roof. With him, she ached, she needed, she wanted. And because she did, she wanted more than anything to make love with him. But whether that happened or not, she knew that sooner or later their game of who owed whom would play itself out.

Strong hands closed over her shoulders and turned her around, and she looked up into Nathan's laughing eyes.

"Congratulations," she said, handing him a cold soda. "The kids love you."

He laughed. "Well, they're pretty great kids with obvious good taste." He upended the soda can and thirstily drank.

She watched him for a moment. "And it doesn't hurt that you're a natural with them."

"I've had a lot of experience these last few years. The Damaron family seems to be growing by leaps and bounds." The hard edges of his face had softened and his eyes were full of humor and light. "For so long it was just me and my cousins. But now we have a whole new generation, and it's wonderful to see all those little ones running around."

"*Nathan.*"

He turned and waved at Dylan, one of the little

boys he'd been playing with. Dylan was gesturing for him to return to their play.

She eyed him solemnly. "Sounds as if you'd like to be a father yourself one day."

"Definitely," he said, his gaze on Dylan. "As far as I'm concerned, the more the better."

A pain stabbed near her heart. She knew exactly what it was like to want babies. She yearned to hold her own baby, feel its chubby little arms around her neck, and be able to breathe in that sweet baby smell. She also knew exactly what it was like to know that she would never experience that kind of happiness.

"*This is my rest period,*" Nathan yelled at Dylan. "*You all play by yourselves for a while.*" Groans filtered up the hill to them. He looked back at her. "And by the way, now *you* owe *me.*"

She couldn't manage a smile, but she strove to keep her tone light. "Oh yeah? How do you figure that?"

"I agreed to help out at a wiener roast, not to be an animal handler."

"I didn't see you having to handle the horse."

"Then you missed quite a lot. That was one mean animal. Really vicious. You didn't see the fight in his eyes like I did."

She laughed. "That was an old horse, and it was one of the gentlest I've ever seen. I wouldn't have hired him otherwise."

Nathan shook his head. "I don't know what horse you thought you were hiring, but *this* horse didn't like children at all. It was me and me alone who protected them. You owe me, Dani, and you owe me big."

"Okay, okay." She knew the horse who had showed up today had been the one she'd initially hired, but for whatever reason, Nathan wanted to extend their game. And heaven help her, she wanted it too. "What did you have in mind as payment?"

"Oh, I don't know. Maybe dinner? Something more substantial than hot dogs. Back at your place."

"Sure," she agreed readily. "Nothing could be easier than dinner."

He leaned forward and pressed a lingering kiss to her lips. "Great," he murmured. "So when are these kids leaving?"

Dani excused herself as soon as they arrived at her apartment. While she washed up, Nathan took the opportunity to explore. The late-afternoon sunlight slanted through tall windows and onto the oak floor. Plants flourished. Books lined oak shelves, along with prominently placed pictures of what he guessed were family and friends. After studying their faces, he turned to a row of humorous little elephants and plaintive-looking donkeys. Then he saw the snow globe with the Eiffel Tower in it. It sat dead center on her mantel.

With a smile, he moved on. Her living room was furnished with a lot of white wicker, plus an enormous, cream-colored sofa, that, from its style and caved-in appearance, he suspected she might have rescued from someone's garbage heap and recovered it with a slipcover.

Suddenly he stopped. In an alcove off the living room hung a large oil painting of a young male dancer. He was dressed for a ballet role in tights, velvet doublet, and white shirt with voluminous sleeves. It was an extraordinary painting done in dreamy pastels, but the sheer joy and exuberance of the young man as he danced showed as clearly as if he were shouting his feelings. He heard Dani behind him and turned.

She'd changed from the jeans and T-shirt she'd worn for the picnic into a red skirt and a white cotton top. Her hair fell loose and shining to the middle of her back. Desire pierced him. His muscles hardened. Heat ran through his veins. He had to turn away from her before he grabbed her and started kissing her.

"Tell me about this painting," he said roughly.

Her gaze softened as she looked at the young boy in the painting. "That's an old friend of mine. His name was Gil Santos. He was a wonderful dancer. He was on his way to being a great dancer."

"Was?"

"He died when he was eighteen in a motorcycle accident."

"I'm sorry."

A soft smile curved her lips. "I am too. There, he's dressed as Prince Siegfried in *Swan Lake*. It was an important production and he loved the role, but it was the last role he danced before his death." She fell silent as she stared at the painting.

"And the painting?" he prodded.

"After Gil's death a friend of ours painted it for me from a photograph."

"This Gil must have been very important to you."

She nodded, her expression hard to read. "Yes, yes, he was. We were in love. Let's go into the kitchen and see what's there."

She swirled and disappeared into the kitchen, leaving him to digest her words. Surprisingly, it was hard. The thought that she'd been in love with this boy Gil didn't sit well with him. Odd that he should mind. After all, Dani was a grown woman. It only made sense that she had a past.

But he supposed what bothered him was that it had been a *meaningful* past. Stupid of him. But hell, she still kept the painting in a central place in her apartment. He'd never been jealous of anything or anyone in his life, but here he was, jealous of a dead boy. He shook his head in disgust at himself.

When he caught up with her, she had the refrigerator door open and was peering in. "So what would you like? Spaghetti and meatballs? Meat loaf and garlic mashed potatoes? Salisbury steak? Salad? Ummm . . ." She bent from her hips with her back perfectly straight and gazed toward the rear of the refrigerator. "Coconut cream pie. Oh, and a small amount of ham with corn."

Nathan leaned back against the counter, his

arms crossed over his chest, enjoying the view of her narrow hips and temptingly curved behind. Enhancing the view was the fact that her skirt was hiked up to just below her bottom. "You have all that in your refrigerator?"

She straightened and turned toward him, and he saw her face again, lovely and calm. A strange lump formed in his throat.

"I told you nothing could be easier than dinner. John, my neighbor across the hall, loves to cook. I love to eat. So we have a deal. He cooks to his heart's content and I eat whatever he cooks. It's a great arrangement for both of us."

His gesture took in the full length of her body. "But you're nothing more than skin, bones, and muscle. How do you eat it all and remain so small?"

She shrugged. "If you taught all the classes I do, day in and day out, and did practically every step your students did three or four times, you'd understand." She waved her hand toward the inside of her refrigerator. "What do you want to eat? John's cooked all of these things this weekend, but the Salisbury steak and coconut cream pie are new since this morning."

"He has a key to your apartment?"

She laughed. "Yes. My refrigerator is very important to John. In fact, when I was ready to go out and buy a new one, he told me exactly what model and size to get."

He stared at her. "Anything else in this apartment that he's attached to?"

"Well, there's me." She flashed him a smile.

"Really." He was silent, as if he was trying to decide what to say next. Finally he said, "None of that food is frozen?"

"No," she said with exaggerated patience meant to tease him. "It's in my *refrigerator*. That means it's not frozen. Now, if it were in my freezer, that would mean it was frozen."

"Uh-huh. But don't you think it's a little unusual to have all that food in there at once? Unless you can eat it all in the next few days, which personally I would consider impossible, it will spoil."

"Which is why I'll keep some of it out and then put the rest of it in the freezer tonight."

He pushed away from the counter and in the next moment had folded his fingers around her upper arms. "You're making fun of me, aren't you?"

"Not at all." She giggled, ruining the effect of what she'd just said. "It's just that I'm fascinated at how a man who I'm sure never shops, cooks, or even puts his own food in the refrigerator, or takes it out, can decide that he's qualified to tell me about food."

"That's not true."

"Which part?"

"I do occasionally take something out of the refrigerator."

"I see," she said as solemnly as possible, but then grinned. "I stand corrected."

He brought her closer to him and nuzzled his face against her neck. "God, you smell good."

Warmth careened through her. Having him in her apartment, in her kitchen, was a new kind of familiarity. Even though it was what she wanted, craved even, she was still overwhelmed by it, by him. His presence was larger than life, his energy immense, and he filled up the small space, making it hard for her to breathe. She gently pulled away. "You're just hungry and it's the food you smell."

Suddenly he slid his hands beneath her arms, lifted, swung her around, and set her down on top of the counter. "If I ever found a food that tasted like you smelled, I'd be eating twenty-four hours a day."

Then he kissed her, a hard, hungry, devouring kiss that stole away her breath and any thought of dinner she might have had. It was incredibly easy to simply go with the feelings he aroused in her, the feelings of need and desire that were all so new to her and kept her so on edge. The pressure of his mouth was firm, the thrust of his tongue demanding. She circled her arms around his neck and held on tightly.

His hands slid up and down her back, then around to her breasts, stroking and caressing until she moaned with delight. He muttered something indecipherable, grabbed her long, slim legs, wrapped them around his waist, and pulled her against him. Her skirt slid to the top of her thighs, but modesty wasn't something she was concerned about at that moment.

His hands soon found the bare skin of her thighs

and his fingers traced daring patterns higher and higher until a finger slipped beneath her panties to the nub nestled between the sensitive, delicate folds of her femininity. There, she began to ache, throb. There, moisture increased. There, she wanted him.

He jerked back. "I think we better have dinner," he said, his voice deep and raw.

"Dinner?" She frowned at him, dazed and uncomprehending.

"Dinner," he said, and turned away. "We need to eat now, because when I start making love to you, I'm not going to stop for a long, long time."

She didn't want to eat. She only wanted him. But she slid off the counter and pressed her hands to her cheeks where she felt heat. "I think we'll have the meat loaf, corn, potatoes, and salad. Does that sound good to you?"

"It will do for now."

FIVE

Dani preceded Nathan up the stairs past the third and fourth floors of her brownstone. At the very top of the last set of stairs, she opened the door and stepped out onto the roof. He followed her, but because it was dark, he could make out only vague shapes.

Then she flipped a switch and thousands of tiny white lights turned on. His first impression was that of a fairyland. Then he realized what he was seeing. It was a rooftop garden burgeoning with hundreds of different shrubs, plants, and trees of all sizes and shapes, growing in everything from large terra-cotta-and-stone pots to wooden and tin containers.

She threw a smile at him over her shoulder. "Like it? It's taken John and me three years to get it to this point."

"It's wonderful," he said, and meant it. He recognized a well-thought-out garden when he saw it.

Some things had been planted for color, such as holly and viburnum. Others had been planted for scent, such as bayberry and mahonia. And still others for texture, such as climbing hydrangea and Japanese silver grass.

"So this is another thing you and John share." He congratulated himself on the fact that his jealousy didn't show in his voice. But he knew somehow he was going to have to get a handle on it, because absurdly, he felt jealous no matter what man she was talking about.

She turned and looked up at him, her expression serious. "John and I are just friends."

Lord, she could see right through him. Only his family had ever been able to do that. He was going to have to be more careful, because if she knew the fierceness of his growing need for her, she'd run screaming from him.

But she must have felt at least a part of his intent, because she executed a perfect *soutenu* turn away from him and toward an area beneath a striped awning. There was a bed there, along with a couple of cushioned chairs. There was also a table, holding, among other things, a CD player.

But he couldn't take his eyes off the bed, made up with a spread of blues and greens, along with matching pillows. "Is that bed left out here year-round? I mean, aren't you afraid it will get ruined up here?"

She shook her head as she riffled through a stack of CDs. "In the winter I take off the bedding and cover it with a tarp, but the rest of the year it's fine. The bed itself is iron and the spread and pillows can be washed if necessary."

He scanned the buildings on either side of them and discovered that with the help of strategically placed trees and hanging screens of flowing fabric, no windows from the other buildings directly over-looked the roof.

His gaze returned to the bed. The moment he'd seen it, images had seared his brain of the two of them making love there, covered only by the sky and moonlight. "What do you do up here?" he asked huskily.

"Oh, just about anything I want. I relax, nap, visit with friends. I even sleep up here a lot during the summer."

"Really?"

She nodded as she slipped several CDs into the player, then pressed a button. Low, melodic music that was a combination of jazz and blues floated out to envelop the rooftop. "I also dance up here. It's one of my favorite places. Sometimes I use it to choreograph the steps I'll teach in my classes, but mostly I like to dance for myself. There's something freeing about this place."

Her eyes glistened with pleasure as she spoke of dancing on the roof. The breeze ruffled her hair around her face. Aching for her, he went toward her.

But unaware of his intentions, she glided past

him on the waves of the music. "Like this," he heard her say.

Riveted, he watched her. Each foot was precisely planted, her elegant back was straight, her head held high. With each measured step, her arms lifted slowly, gracefully. Then she rose on tiptoe and *bourrées* propelled her across the rooftop, her feet moving so swiftly and in such tiny steps that she fairly floated, her skirt wafting out around her.

The music was an instrumental, but she was the lyrics, he thought. And as the music reached a high note she stepped onto one foot to perform a perfectly arched arabesque. Nathan held his breath as she balanced, arms *allongé*, reaching for the stars, with one leg raised, its toe pointed upward, copying the line of her arm.

How many seconds did he forget to breathe? he wondered. He had no idea. He was completely enchanted.

As the music fell away she executed a *renversé* that had him raising his hands to catch her. No one could keep her balance in such a spiraling move. But then miraculously she was facing him, her smile soft and beckoning. He didn't think she was seeing him, though. She was lost in the music. She *was* the music.

She poised again on flat, dipped into a *penché*, and as she came up she raised one hand to— Whom? Whom was she seeing? He remembered the prince in the painting. Did she dance up here alone for Siegfried, for Gil Santos?

Even if she did, it didn't matter. For once he wasn't jealous. *He* was the man who was with her tonight and he planned to make sure that she would always remember their time here together. For some reason it was important to him that from now on he wanted her to think of only him when she danced.

Dani continued to flow together with the music. She was a dream and she was reality. He was fascinated by her suppleness and the elegant poetry of her every move. He was bewitched by her spontaneity and passion. She arched her body in ways he wouldn't have thought possible, and at that moment she stepped into a series of exquisite adagio movements *à une*.

Her unconscious sensuality left him throbbing and needy. If he didn't have her soon . . .

She danced past him again and this time he reached out, caught her wrist, and brought her against him. Her face was flushed, her hair disheveled, her breathing quick. He bent his head and crushed his lips down on hers, hot and forceful.

She responded, returning his kiss with eagerness, opening her mouth wider, meeting his seeking tongue with her own. And she pressed against him, her pliant body a miracle to him. His shaking hands sought out the perfect shape of her breasts, and his thumbs flicked over her nipples. She moaned with pleasure.

Then with no warning, she went rigid in his arms.

"What?" he asked, his voice raw with the heated emotions he was feeling. "What's wrong?"

She pulled away from him. Her mouth parted, but no words came out.

"What's wrong?" he asked again, smoothing her long hair away from her face. "Is it me? Is it something I did?"

"No."

Frustrated, he ran his fingers through his hair. "Dani, you come apart in my arms when I kiss you. I want you and I know you want me. Why are you pulling away? Obviously there's something wrong. Tell me what it is and we'll talk about it."

She shook her head. "God, I feel like such a fool."

"Why?" He was hard, his body throbbing. He was in no condition to think straight, but he was trying. Lord, he was trying.

"I'm sorry."

"Forget sorry. Just tell me."

She drew in a deep breath. "Okay. I think it's important for you to know that I haven't had many boyfriends. In fact . . . I've had only one."

"One?" With a knuckle beneath her chin, he lifted her face.

"Gil."

"The boy in the painting."

"Yes."

"Okay," he said slowly, reaching for patience that wasn't there. His body was clamoring for her, his nerves were hurting, and what she was saying didn't make sense to him.

She stared up at him. "It's just that I'm not experienced—not at all—and certainly not to the point that I'm sure you're used to. But because I threw myself at you that night on the quay, you probably have the exact opposite opinion of me. So I wanted to tell you."

He smiled. "My opinion of you, Dani, is that you're amazing and that I'm an extremely lucky man because you chose me that night."

"Thank you."

Something was still bothering her. It was there in the depths of her eyes. He took her hand, drew her to the bed, and pulled her down beside him. "Now tell me. Do you feel I'm rushing you? If so, I'm sorry." He paused, thinking. "No, I take that back. I'm not sorry. I want you. And I think you want me. Am I wrong?"

"No, you're not." She laughed hollowly. "And if you'd asked me this afternoon, I would have said I was ready for this evening. But here I am with cold feet."

Breath rasped in and out of his lungs as he tried to reassure her. "It's all right."

"It's incredibly stupid," she murmured, shaking her head. "But right at this moment I suddenly feel overwhelmed."

"By what? Who?"

"*You.* You overwhelm me, Nathan. I imagine you overwhelm most ordinary people."

He couldn't help but smile. "Well, there's your problem. You think you're ordinary. But let me tell you, you couldn't be more wrong. If you think you're ordinary, then you're definitely not seeing what I'm seeing."

She looked away. "You know, you didn't misread me, Nathan. I do want you."

"Good, because I'm not used to going slow. When I want something, I go after it."

A smile slowly banished her doubt-filled expression. "I know that about you."

He lifted her hand and pressed a kiss to its back. "What I'm trying to say is that if you need me to, I'll do my best to go slowly. Or at least as slowly as I can. And if it makes you feel better, I promise you that nothing will happen that you don't want to happen."

She chuckled. "That's a loaded promise that's filled with the potential to be very dangerous."

"Meaning what?"

"Meaning you can sweep me away with only a kiss, and before I know it, I'll want *everything* to happen."

His laugh was shaky. "You really shouldn't be telling me that."

"It's the truth."

God in heaven, she got to him. He looked down at her hand in his, small with clear, oval-shaped nails. "You keep saying things like that and I won't be able to keep my promise."

"What promise?" she asked softly. She reached

out and with a hand on his chin, turned him to face her. "Kiss me."

"But you said—"

"I said, kiss me."

Without another word, he brought his lips down on hers. The sweetness was there. And the clawing need, so strong he was nearly dizzy with it. There was so much going on inside of him. Urges as old as time. Touches of magic completely new to him. Emotions he couldn't define. Heat for which there was no relief.

Gently he smoothed his hand along the side of her face, then down her neck. His fingers found the pulse point at the base of her throat, pressed and felt its rapid cadence. It matched his own.

Her skin was warm, soft, and perfumed. He skimmed his lips back up her neck to her mouth and thrust his tongue deep into her. And it was like coming home. It had all started between them with a kiss. And now it would continue.

As he kissed her his fingers trailed lower to the neckline of her top and pushed it off her shoulder so that he could slide his hand beneath it to cup one small, perfect breast. Electricity scored through him.

Her effect on him was amazing. She made him want her, and even now when he was about to take her, he knew it wouldn't be enough. She was like a banquet to a man who hadn't known he was starving until he looked at her. And he knew, the more he had of her, the more he would want.

"I can't go slow anymore," he muttered.

"Good," she whispered. "I'm ready for fast."

A moan escaped her mouth and found its way into his. He wasted no more time. He slipped her top up and over her head, then cupped his hand around her breast and slid his palm back and forth over her nipple. She reacted immediately, urgently circling her arms around his neck and pulling him against her.

Blood roared in his ears and he eased her back onto the bed. Despite what she'd said about being ready, he tried to take it slow. She might be ready for fast, but since she hadn't been with a man for nine years, it was only reasonable to expect that her body would need time to adapt to his. At least that's what his head told him, but his body was saying something different, urging him to action. He released her breast, then smoothed his hand under her skirt.

With one motion he stripped her panties from her. Then he began to stroke her with his fingers, finding sensitive spots that made her moan and twist and arch beneath his hand. She was moist; she was ready for him. He slipped a finger into her and felt her shudder. A savage pressure was building inside him. He was so hard, it was almost pain.

"Make love to me," she whispered. "Now."

The words pierced deep to the most primitive part of him. With a ragged groan his hand went to his belt. "Undressing all the way is going to have to wait."

Within moments he was over her. Flexing his hips, he pressed his erection against the nub hidden in the folds of her sex. She gasped, arching her back, then he thrust into her, pushing deeper and deeper until he filled her up entirely. With a cry of ecstasy, she wrapped her arms around his neck and her legs around his back.

She moved with him, matching his rhythm exactly as he plunged in and out of her, fast and hard, desperate to put out the fire that gripped him. He wanted release from the intense pleasure that coiled ever tighter, making it hard for him to breathe. He wanted it to last forever.

No other woman had ever made him feel this way, he thought hazily. She was velvet, she was fire. She was perfumed skin, she was red-hot passion. With her slight, strong body, she was taking him to heights he'd never known existed. Even as he was possessing her she was driving him crazy with need.

Then, beneath him, she stiffened and cried out. At the same time his body convulsed and he erupted into her. A red-hot sweetness burned through him, hurtling him toward darkness and light, leaving him scorched, spent, and deeply satisfied.

The moon had climbed high in the sky, serene and fathomless. Lying beneath it with Nathan, Dani felt a wonder she'd never known before, and at the same time, a concern.

His chest rose and fell as he dozed, but even in

sleep, his strong arms kept her cradled against him. She lay very still, content that he slept. The respite from their passion gave her a much-needed opportunity to see if she could put what had happened between them into some sort of context that made sense.

Her only other sexual experience had been with Gil. With him, she'd first become his friend. Then gradually she'd fallen in love with him and he with her. And it had all been incredibly easy. There'd been no emotional upheavals, no great rush of passion to the heights, no dizzying free falls.

But there was all of that and more with Nathan. He affected her like a thunderbolt out of the night sky. Being near him was like holding a grenade in her hand, its pin already pulled. The potential for danger was just a breath away. One slip of her finger off the lever and there would be an explosion of a magnitude from which she might not ever recover.

As there'd been tonight.

She eased a few inches away from Nathan and angled her head along his arm so that she could look at him. He had the strongest jaw and the longest eyelashes of any man she'd ever known. He would be a formidable opponent no matter what the game, yet here she was, playing a game with him of his own making, his own rules.

His hair . . . Lightly she traced a finger along the silver streak. He was a man who had the power to rearrange the world if he didn't like what he saw. What was a woman like her doing in his arms? A woman who adjusted to the world rather than trying to change it.

The answer came to her immediately. Because there was no other place she wanted to be.

Earlier, right before they made love, she had balked. She'd told him that she was overwhelmed by him. It hadn't been the truth exactly, but it also hadn't been a complete lie. She'd balked because she'd known that when she finally made love with him, her whole world would change. A last-ditch effort at self-protection, she supposed. But she'd failed at it.

She hadn't been able to stop their lovemaking. Like the moon's pull on the tides, it had been inevitable. She'd gone into his arms and made soul-destroying, mind-bending love to him. And because she had, nothing would ever be the same.

She loved him.

She didn't know when she'd fallen in love, or at what exact moment she'd crossed the line from attraction to love, but she did know she'd well and truly fallen in love with him.

She had to be crazy, she told herself. Yet she'd had no choice. Falling in love with Nathan had happened without her knowledge or consent. In retrospect, it sounded so simple. Unfortunately, it was anything but.

He caught her hand and drew it from his hair down to his chest.

"You're awake," she said softly.

"I was never really asleep. Your thinking kept me awake."

"My thinking?"

He chuckled, a deep rumble in his chest. "I could practically hear your mind working."

She grinned, happy and content in the moment. "And did you hear *what* I was thinking?"

He rolled off his back to his side, then brushed a strand of hair off her cheek. "Not exactly, but I have a pretty good guess."

Her grin faded. "Really?" It was entirely possible that he did know what she'd been thinking, that he'd guessed she loved him. It was possible because she was certain that practically every woman he slept with fell in love with him. She was sure he even had a pat response for letting them down gently. She waited to hear what it was.

"You're upset because I didn't think to use protection. I'm upset too."

He'd surprised her. Truthfully she hadn't thought about protection either.

He sat up and leaned back against the cushions. "I owe you a big apology, Dani."

"No, you don't," she murmured, and pushed herself up in the bed until she was beside him.

"Are you kidding?" He ran his fingers through his hair. "I don't know exactly what happened. I *always* use protection, but with you . . ." He shook his head with a mixture of disgust and bewilderment. "I had to have you and I couldn't wait."

"I'm not upset," she said carefully. She under-

stood how he could have forgotten. The fire between them had been too hot to allow for thought.
"It's all right, really. I told you there hasn't been
another man since Gil and I didn't lie. There's absolutely no chance of a disease of any kind." She
paused. "And as for the risk of my getting pregnant,
there's no risk."

He frowned at her. "Are you sure?"

"I'm positive."

"Then you're on the pill," he said, and she
heard the relief in his voice.

She hesitated. "Something like that."

"Something like that?"

"Nathan, I assure you there's no chance I will
become pregnant."

"Then you forgive me?" She nodded. "Thank
God." He leaned over and pressed a kiss to her
forehead, then one to her lips. "Oh, but one last
thing."

"What?"

"I'm also clean when it comes to disease."

She'd never doubted it. He was a man who
would be in total control of all aspects of his life.
She believed him when he said it wasn't the norm
for him to forget about protection.

He slipped lower down the pillows, pulled her
down with him, and angled his body toward her. He
took her breast in his hand. Clearly his mind had
already moved back to sex.

"I'm afraid I have a ballerina's body," she said,
surprising herself. Like most dancers, she'd never

been self-conscious about her body, but with him, now, she wanted her curves to be fuller, more desirable. "No breasts."

"They're perfect," he said huskily, and bent his head to draw in one aching tip and suckle.

A sound erupted from her and she arched against him as heated sensations hit her with the force of a hurricane wind. Lord, she must seem incredibly easy to him, but there was nothing she could do about her response. She'd never learned to hide her feelings. She'd never had to.

He lifted his head, his eyes already drowsy with passion, and he skimmed his hands over her stomach. "Your body is fascinating to me. It's a flawless blend of muscles and grace, with nothing superfluous." His fingers delved lower between her legs, lightly rubbing.

She could feel herself descending into a drugged state of heated desire where nothing else mattered but the passion and the urgency for the satisfaction to come. She'd already been there once tonight. It was a place she wanted to go again.

"I'm not accustomed to losing control," he muttered, sliding his body closer to hers, his muscles tight with intent, his erection hard against her thigh. "But I did with you." His fingers slipped in and out of her.

She had no idea what to say, and even if she could think of something, her heart was racing so fast, she could barely breathe.

While his fingers moved in her he leaned over

and placed a long, deep kiss to her mouth. "But I've had you now. I won't lose control again."

Need was twisting and coiling inside her stomach, fire was converging between her legs, and his loss of control couldn't have been less important to her. His relentless stroking had her silken inner flesh inflamed.

"Nathan." His name was an urgent plea. Desperate for some kind of grounding, she reached out for him, slipping her arm around his neck, but he wouldn't yield. Her hips began to undulate of their own accord.

"Do you have any idea how beautiful you are at this moment, how incredibly desirable you are to me?"

She was past any answer. Her head thrashed back and forth on the pillow as she felt something in her body lift and begin to climb. She cried out. Then she was soaring on the gust of a powerful climax and all she could do was try to hold on to him.

But he offered her no safe haven. "*God, I want you.*"

The words came to her from a distance and they sounded angry and rough. Even as she was descending from her climax he moved over her, parted her legs, and drove into her. With his next thrust, she took off again with a startled cry. She climbed up and up and then even higher until there was nothing but Nathan and a brilliant, blinding passion.

"I'm taking you to Helene's tomorrow."

She didn't think she could have moved if her life had depended on it. She was completely sated and exhausted. She drew in a deep breath, the first deep breath she'd been able to draw since they'd begun to make love. "There's no need," she finally managed. "I'll find my own way." She half hoped he wouldn't go with her, she realized. With him there she might not be able to concentrate on the task at hand. Yet she also half hoped he would go. It would give her another chance to spend a little more time with him.

"You may not think there's a need, but I do. The money Helene's promised us if you can help Cecilia will do enormous good. I'm just going along to protect my investment, that's all."

She drew in another deep breath, hoping for energy. "You sound angry."

"Angry?" He stirred beside her, then rolled over so that his body was pressed tightly along the length of hers. "No, of course I'm not angry." He slid one long leg over hers in a most possessive manner. "Why should I be angry? You and I just had some of the most fabulous sex I've ever had."

He was definitely angry about something. His voice carried a razor-sharp edge. The seemingly endless ride of climaxes he'd taken her on had left her devoid of practically all thought, yet there was something he'd said. . . . What had it been?

When had he said it? Minutes ago? Or maybe it had been an hour ago. Oh, she had it. Something about losing control with her. And then he had. But what did it matter?

She really knew only one thing. To her, what she'd experienced in his arms had been transcendent lovemaking. Yet to him, it had been only fabulous sex. But that was okay. She understood and accepted his feelings, even if it did leave a sharp ache in her heart. He hadn't asked her to love him, even though she did, and he had certainly never promised to love her in return, which was fine. It was. Really.

"I'm taking you to Helene's."

"Okay," she whispered, too exhausted to argue with him.

In the next moment he did a strange thing for an angry man. He reached for the covers and brought them up to wrap around the two of them. Then he pulled her into his arms and gently brushed the hair from her face. "Sleep," he whispered.

And she did.

SIX

"So, anyway, I'm waiting for Nathan to take me to Helene Sorge's. I don't know what possessed me to offer to help her granddaughter, but before I knew it, my mouth had opened and the words had come out." Gazing down on the street from her front window, Dani stood balanced on her right foot, the left resting on the opposite leg, the portable phone cradled between her shoulder and ear.

Her sister laughed warmly. "Sounds just like you. It's that impetuous nature of yours, plus your desire to help others."

"I know, but, Natalie, Helene Sorge told me she'd consulted top specialists on her granddaughter's behalf. If they couldn't help her, how can I expect that I can?"

"Because you're you and the specialists aren't."

She chuckled. "I'm sure there's logic somewhere in what you just said, but darned if I can find it. Oh, but what about the money for the new children's wing she promised? What if I can't help the girl? Helene won't donate the money unless I do."

"Don't let that put you under any pressure. Naturally the Damarons want to raise as much outside money as possible, but if push comes to shove, they'll fork over the extra funds needed."

Dani switched feet, balancing now on her left foot. She reached out to pull back the white sheer curtain. Still no sign of Nathan. "I suppose you're right."

"I am. So, okay, *give.* I can't wait any longer. Tell me how things are going between you and Nathan."

"How things are going?" She deliberately repeated the question to give herself time to think about her answer.

"You're stalling, Dani."

"I'm thinking, Natalie."

"Well, stop it and tell."

Dani let the sheer drop back into place. "I'm in love with him."

Stunned silence filled her ear. Then: "Oh, honey . . ."

"I know. You don't have to say anything. Believe me, I know exactly how stupid it is, but I didn't have a choice. It just happened."

"Well, okay, so it happened. Okay . . ."

Natalie was obviously trying to think her way through the situation and was having a tough time, Dani thought ruefully. She understood.

"Well, I don't think it's necessarily a *bad* thing. Not at all. In fact . . . hmmm . . . here's what I think. It's *wonderful*. Truly. And for goodness' sakes, he's a *Damaron*. I know there's that rumor that they're heartbreakers, but once you get past that, everything is good. In fact, from what I understand, there's not a bad one in the lot."

Dani grinned. "He's definitely not bad. In fact, in our short acquaintance I can say unequivocally that he's wonderful. The problem is, he doesn't love me."

"Good grief, Dani. Give him *time*. You haven't even known each other a week yet. I can see why you'd fall in love quickly. You've always been impetuous and your emotions have always run close to the surface. But as for him, most men are commitment shy, and a Damaron would have more reason than most to be. He's got all that money to protect, and he'd have to be assured that you're not a fortune hunter."

Dani blinked. "Why would he think that?"

Her sister laughed. "Surely you can't have forgotten so soon. Remember? When you *threw* yourself at him?"

She bit her bottom lip. "Yeah, okay, so I did."

"See? But once he really gets to know you and realizes you're not after his money . . ."

She sighed. "It doesn't matter, Nat. This isn't going to work out. In fact, I plan for today to be the last time I see him."

"*What?* Are you crazy? Why would you want to

do something that stupid? You just said you loved him."

A car pulled up out front. Dani's foot hit the floor and her pulse quickened with excitement. Then she saw John bound out of the building to talk to a couple she could now see in the car.

"I told you why. Because it's not going to work out."

"And I told you. Give it time. He'll come to love you. Why wouldn't he? You're wonderful."

She smiled. "And of course, you're not one bit biased."

"Not a bit."

"Oh, Natalie—it's just not that simple. I may love Nathan, but he's not a part of my everyday life yet, and his departure from it wouldn't even leave a hole in my days and nights."

"Do you really believe that?"

She nodded her head, then shook it. "Well, sort of. But what I'm really trying to forestall is a hole in my *heart*. When he leaves, I know there'll be one, but at this stage I'm hoping that it will be a *small* hole."

"Now, I *know* you don't believe that. Dani, look, I don't know why you don't think it will work out between you two—you and I will have a longer talk as soon as you have more time—but until then, don't make any hasty decisions."

"I—" Another car pulled to a stop behind John's friends. Seconds later Nathan climbed out. "He's here. I need to go."

"All right, but just remember what I said. Oh, and Dani? Enjoy today."

Dani grimaced. "Enjoying myself when I'm with Nathan doesn't seem to be a problem."

She hit the disconnect button, scooped up her purse, and raced downstairs.

As she stepped out the door she heard John's friendly voice. "Hi. You here to pick up Dani?" He waved to his friends as they drove away.

"That's right," Nathan replied guardedly.

"She'll be right down. Oh, here she is now."

Nathan turned to see Dani, her bare legs practically flying down the stairs, her hair done up, her short, pink dress flaring above her knees. Heat stirred in his loins. He would have thought after the night they'd spent that his body would have been sated by now, but no. He'd awakened at dawn, wanting her more than ever. They'd made love and now he wanted her again.

"Nathan," she said as soon as she reached his side, "this is John. John, this is Nathan."

John immediately extended his hand and Nathan took it. Then, very deliberately, Nathan put his arm around Dani and drew her against him. She came easily, her lips curved in a soft smile. Unable to resist, he bent and pressed a light kiss to her lips. The sweetness almost did him in and he was very aware of John's interested gaze. The man annoyed him. His presence was keeping him from doing more than just lightly kissing Dani.

He looked down at her. She had a light pink

rose in her hair, a rose that looked as if it had been picked from one of the rosebushes on the roof garden. For a moment it distracted him, because it brought back a myriad of heated memories they'd shared there last night and this morning. He wanted to say something personal to Dani about the rose, but he didn't want to embarrass her in front of John.

Still, he put his mouth to Dani's ear. "Pretty rose." She smiled up at him and he could barely keep himself from kissing her again.

He turned his attention to John and actively looked for a reason to dislike him. "So you're the cook."

John roared with laughter. "Dani told me you two ate the meat loaf. How'd you like it?"

"It was quite good," he said grudgingly. "I gather cooking is a hobby rather than a vocation?"

John grinned good-naturedly. "Cooking is a compulsion, but computer programming is my business."

"He works out of his apartment," Dani volunteered.

"Really. So you and Dani both work out of the brownstone. Must be nice to have your neighbor so close."

"We help each other out."

"Sometimes I don't know what I would do without John," Dani said with a cute smile, and a wrinkled nose at her neighbor. "He helps me in so many ways."

Nathan was liking the man less and less. "Besides keeping your refrigerator stocked, you mean?"

"Oh, sure. For one thing, he moves my furniture around when I get in the mood."

"Dani has delusions of grandeur," John said in a confiding voice that grated on Nathan's nerves. "She thinks she's strong enough not only to move furniture, but to lift an adult student when there's been an injury. I call it her Hercules complex."

Their ease with each other indicated endless hours spent together. Dammit. Trying to be fair, though, he decided that it wasn't John's fault that he'd only just found Dani. But now that he had, he decided it was time John backed off.

Playfully, Dani hit John's arm with the back of her hand and Nathan gave him a thin smile.

"Isn't it a little boring, John, staying home all the time?" John had entirely too much time to spend with Dani. He needed to get out and have a normal job like most people.

The other man grinned. "*If* I stayed home all the time, it might be. But for starters, there's a rule of thumb. He who cooks a lot must go to the grocery store a lot."

Nathan felt a tug on his arm and looked down at Dani. "We should get going," she said. "I'd hate to keep Helene waiting."

"Fine." He glanced back at John, who had a small smile playing around his lips. "Nice to have met you," he said, trying his best to infuse his tone with sincerity.

"Right. You too."

When it came to his dislike of John, he was in the wrong, Nathan reflected. Yet he couldn't help but feel relief and more than a little satisfaction as he ushered Dani into his car and away from John. Then for good measure he locked the door after her. His reaction was beyond strange, he admitted to himself. Dani herself had told him she and John were simply friends, and truthfully he could see no evidence to the contrary. Maybe next time he'd try a little harder to be nicer to John. Dani would like that and what Dani liked was becoming more and more important to him.

At first he concentrated on the traffic, but as soon as he could, he looked over at her. Before, he'd only noticed that her hair was up and that it had the pink rose in it. Now he saw what she'd done.

Starting high on her head, she'd French-braided her long brown hair on both sides. When she'd reached the nape of her neck, she'd taken the two braids and woven them into one. At the bottom of the braid, she secured it, then rolled it under until she could tuck it into the original braids and pin it into place.

As for the rose, she'd actually braided it into her hair on the left side so that it hung just below her earlobe. Very witchy, very alluring. And on her ears, she wore small, delicate drop earrings that added to the allure.

"I like your hair," he said huskily. "It gives you a . . . regal look."

She chuckled. "This is the way I usually wear my hair when I'm dancing or teaching. It keeps it in place."

"I like it, but then I also like your hair when it's down."

"Thank you for noticing."

He heard the touch of surprise in her voice as he took a left turn. He smiled. When it came to her, she had no idea how much he noticed. "Did you get any sleep after I left this morning?"

She shook her head. "I went ahead and got up. I had things to do. I've already taught three classes today."

"Three? You must be tired."

"Not at all." She looked around her. "You know, I didn't think to ask where Helene lives. Is it far?"

He grinned. "You might say that. We're heading for her estate in Connecticut."

"*Connecticut?*"

He grinned over at her. "Don't worry. I'm taking you back to the Tower and we're going to catch a helicopter from there."

"Oh, Nathan, I'm so sorry. I had no idea this would turn out to be so much trouble for you."

"I'm glad to do it. After all, you are doing this for our family's foundation."

"But Connecticut. I didn't realize. . . . This isn't good. Even if Cecilia is amenable to taking lessons from me, there's no way I can commute to

Connecticut two or three times a week to teach her."

"Why don't we wait and see what happens. If this works out, Helene may decide to move to her city apartment during the week."

"Well, if that's an option and she wouldn't mind doing it . . ." Tiny lines of worry marked her face.

"Hey," he said softly. "Don't worry about it. If it's meant to work out, it will."

She leveled a curious gaze on him. "That's an interesting thing for you to say. You don't seem to be the kind of man who would approach many things in life so passively."

"I don't." He shot her a grin. "But from my viewpoint, everything is going great."

Helene's garden and grounds were much like the woman herself—formal, impeccably groomed, and restrained. As far as Dani could see, there wasn't so much as a blade of grass growing the wrong way. Nevertheless, she was grateful for the grounds because it gave her the opportunity to get Cecilia away from her grandmother and off by themselves, though she was still very aware that Helene and Nathan sat on the back terrace, watching them as they walked.

"Cecilia, your grandmother has told me that your mother studied ballet for years and that she'd loved it so much, she had started you in ballet too."

"Uh-huh."

Cecilia was a thin, shy child, and even though Cecilia's reluctance to have anything to do with her had been obvious from the outset, Dani hadn't had a bit of trouble warming to her. It had been the little girl's eyes, really, that had gotten to her. They were brown and incredibly sad. No child should know that much sadness.

"That's wonderful. That means you're not a beginner any longer. You already know the basic steps." Cecilia didn't say anything. "Do you remember them?"

"No."

"Well, don't worry. They'll come back to you quite easily, you'll see."

"I don't want to take ballet."

It was the first full sentence she'd uttered since they'd started their walk.

"Why not?"

"Because ballet is stupid."

"Stupid? Really? I've always thought ballet was incredibly fun." When Cecilia didn't respond, Dani went on. "Your grandmother and I thought it might be something you'd enjoy doing again. Besides, ballet will put strength into your legs. In fact, it will make you strong all over and maybe even get rid of a lot of the aches and pains you have. Don't you think that would be nice?"

"No."

Dani reached out and lightly touched Cecilia's arm. "Let's go this way." She led the little girl out of the garden and onto the thick, grassy lawn. Not too far away from the garden, she stopped, folded her legs, and sank onto the grass. Then she patted the ground in front of her. "Come join me." After an obvious hesitation Cecilia dropped down with her.

The sun was warm on Dani's face and the wind gently stirred her skirt, but the sad thing was that the little girl sitting before her probably couldn't get past her hurt to notice what a nice day it was. Her heart stirred with sympathy.

"You know what, Cecilia? I know how you feel. I truly do."

Defiance shone in her brown eyes. "No, you don't."

"Yes, honey, I do. You see, when I was eighteen, a boy I loved very much was killed in an awful accident, just as your mom and dad were. And just as you were in the accident with your parents, I was in the accident with him." Cecilia looked up at her with the first signs of interest she'd shown.

Encouraged, Dani went on. "One moment my boyfriend and I were together and happy and everything was perfect. The next he was gone and I was left all alone to cope with some serious injuries and a lot of pain. Many people showed up and tried to help me. My parents. My sister. My friends. But they couldn't help me with my pain. No one could. I just wanted everyone to go away."

"That's what I want."

"I know just how you feel. And you know what else? The pain my body felt after the accident was nothing compared with the pain I felt on the inside. My heart felt as if it was breaking. Is that how you're feeling too?"

Cecilia didn't answer, though her eyes remained steady on her. Dani waited, giving the young girl time to absorb what she'd said so far. "And to make it worse, I even lost the baby that was growing inside me." That was something she rarely told people, but in Cecilia's case she'd decided to make an exception.

"A baby," Cecilia whispered. "That's so sad."

"Yes, yes it was. I honestly thought I'd never get over the pain. So you see, honey, I do know what you're going through. For a long time after the accident, I was angry and most of all I was frightened. I didn't understand why the accident had to have happened and I hated feeling all alone."

Cecilia looked away. "Grandmother tells me I should smile and be happy."

Moved by the soft words, she reached out and gently combed her fingers through the little girl's fine blond hair. "Your grandmother is feeling all the same things you are. She's very, very sad, because when you lost your mother, she lost her daughter. And all she has left is you and she wants more than anything for you to be happy. The thing is, she doesn't know how to be happy any more than you do." She paused. "It would be really nice if you could help your grandmother, don't you think?"

"I don't know how."

"You know what helped me the most to get over

my sadness?" Cecilia shook her head. "I decided I would get well and then I would help others, which is what I do now. I help people have fun through teaching them ballet. That might sound silly, but it's worked for me."

The little girl shook her head again. "I can't teach ballet."

"No, but you can do other things. For instance, you could tell your grandmother that you understand how sad she is and that if she ever wants to talk about it, you'll be there for her."

More than likely Helene had made the exact opposite suggestion to her granddaughter, then waited for Cecilia to talk. But if Helene would start talking about her loss, Cecilia might join in.

"You could also show her you love her by doing little things for her, even if it's only bringing her a bouquet of flowers or taking a glass of water to her. And you could help her even more by trying to get well. That would make her really happy. And there's one more thing that helped me. *Dancing.* Whenever I'm sad or lonely and no one else is around, I dance out what I feel. Do you understand what I'm saying?"

"No."

"Then whenever you want me to, I'll show you." Dani smiled at her. She'd thrown a lot at the little girl. It was time to back off a bit. "You have very pretty hair."

Cecilia looked at her. "You do too. I . . . I like the rose."

Dani's smile broadened. "I tell you what. Why don't you go pick a rose and bring it back. I'll fix your hair just like mine."

"Really?" Dani nodded. "I'll be right back."

When Cecilia came hurrying back with the rose in her hand, she had a new light in her eyes. Dani pulled the young girl down to her and impulsively hugged her. The sweet, tentative smile she received in return was her reward and told her that Helene needed to start hugging her granddaughter. She made a mental note to try to find a tactful way to tell her, then hid a grin at the thought of the frosty reception she would no doubt get.

Positioning Cecilia between her stretched-out legs, she began to braid her hair. She took her time and talked about her love of ballet and how dance had helped her after Gil's death. She was rewarded when Cecilia asked a few questions about her classes.

On their return trip to the house, Dani took a chance and reached for Cecilia's hand, and was delighted when she didn't pull away. But she was really happy when, after reaching the terrace, Cecilia ran to show her hair to her grandmother. Helene appeared to be very touched.

Dani looked out the window of the helicopter to see houses, trees, roads, and occasional bits of water flash beneath the aircraft as it flew them back to New York City. It was dizzying and she found it much easier to fix her eyes on the horizon. It had been a long, fairly satisfying day so far, but the hardest part of it loomed ahead, the part where she'd say good-bye to Nathan.

Sitting next to her in the passenger compartment, he reached over and took her hand.

"You should have seen Helene's face when you sat down with her granddaughter in the middle of that sloping lawn."

She frowned. "What's wrong with sitting on the ground with a child?"

He chuckled. "Not a thing. It's just I doubt it's ever occurred to her to do anything like that, even with her daughter. And then when she saw you reach out for Cecilia and run your fingers through her hair, then hug her, she brushed away a tear."

She slowly shook her head in sympathy with the woman. "Both Helene and Cecilia are in a bad place right now."

"I think you accomplished a miracle today."

Dani looked down at their two hands. Nathan's hand was so much bigger, it completely engulfed hers. Symbolic, really, she thought ruefully. It wasn't that she'd been overwhelmed by him as a man, or by who he was. But she had been overwhelmed by the feelings she felt every time she looked at him and every time she felt his hands or mouth on her.

Truthfully she was deeply affected by everything about him as a man, as a lover, and as the person she was going to have to say good-bye to very soon now.

She sighed. "No, not a miracle. This is going to take a while, but at least I got Cecilia to say she'd come to a class. She's a little girl who's silently crying out for help and affection. Helene instinctively knows it, she just doesn't know how to go about giving her what she needs, or even breaking through to her. I think that's why she agreed to let me come talk to Cecilia today."

"And you knew how to reach her."

She shrugged. "Well, I've had a lot of experience teaching girls her age."

"It has to be something more than that."

Once again she looked down at their entwined hands. "I suffered a similar tragedy in my life, losing someone I loved in an accident—"

"Gil?"

She nodded. "And I was injured in the same accident."

"You didn't tell me that."

She shrugged. "It's not something I talk about a lot, but I did tell Cecilia. I thought it would help her relate to me better."

"Wait. Get back to the part about your being in the accident with Gil. How badly were you injured?"

"There were some significant injuries. Plus, I lost a baby I didn't know I was carrying."

"God, Dani, I'm so sorry."

"It's all right. I worked hard and eventually was

able to heal. And I did make a life-changing decision afterward. I decided to teach instead of dancing professionally as I had been doing."

"I'm sorry," he said, squeezing her hand. "The accident that took Gil was a double hit for you. It must have made it twice as hard on you."

She silently nodded. Actually the accident had been a triple hit for her, but there was no point in telling him about the baby she'd lost. "I was much older than Cecilia when my accident happened. At that age I had certain coping skills, but even then it was nearly impossible to see beyond my loss." She shook her head. "Poor little thing. Cecilia is so young, she doesn't know the first thing about coping. I can only imagine how hurt and scared she's been since it happened. And alone. She's needed so much from Helene, but Helene has been caught up in her own grief."

He lifted her hand and pressed a kiss to her palm. "I'd say it was Helene's lucky day when you walked up to her Saturday night."

She smiled at him. "Actually it was *my* lucky day. You always get more than you give when you help someone. That's what I was trying to tell Cecilia. I just hope I truly will be able to help her."

"Helene certainly thinks you can. She was so impressed with you and what you accomplished with Cecilia today, she wrote me out a check for the amount that she had promised."

Her eyes widened with shock. "I didn't know that."

He patted the breast pocket of his jacket. "I've got it right here."

"Frankly I'm surprised Helene went ahead and wrote the check. I thought she planned to wait and see how Cecilia did after a few lessons."

"Well, whatever her reason, I'm just glad she did."

He sighed dramatically and Dani eyed him curiously. "What?"

"I suppose you know what this check means, don't you?"

The twinkle in his eyes distracted her. "That your foundation now has more money?"

"Yeah, that, too, but it also means that *I* now owe *you*."

She hadn't seen it coming and she didn't know whether to laugh or cry. For whatever reason— whether it was because he wanted to, or because he felt he really did owe her—he wanted to continue their game. More than he would ever know, she wanted to say, *great*. She couldn't, though. "That's not necessary."

"What are you talking about? Of course it's necessary."

"I tell you what. Since this one was for charity, I'll let it go."

He eyed her curiously. "Doesn't matter who or what it's for, or even what the prize is. It could be a snow globe or help with a picnic or a dinner. The point is that if it hadn't been for you and your efforts, I wouldn't have this check in my pocket to deposit tomorrow into the Damaron Foundation account."

"Nathan—"

He put his finger to her lips. "Have I told you that you looked adorable this afternoon out on the lawn, sitting on the grass with that beautiful straight back of yours, practically holding the little girl in your lap as you braided her hair? I wish I'd had a camera."

She'd never known she could be so weak. More than she'd ever thought it possible to want, she wanted to be with him tonight. Maybe tomorrow her courage would return, but this evening it was nowhere in sight.

He squeezed her hand. "Where have you gone?"

She looked at him. "Nowhere. I'm right here with you."

At least for tonight.

SEVEN

"What's it like to live in the sky?" Dani asked.

His apartment was on one of the top floors of the Damaron Tower, his office several floors below. From where she stood at the window, she could see the city spread out before her with its millions of lights. The effect was like an aerial fairyland for the gods.

"Oh, I don't know. I suppose it's quiet and convenient."

"Quiet and convenient? This apartment, this view, they're nothing short of *spectacular*."

He chuckled. "I'm glad you like them."

"Like them? Nathan, you are a very jaded individual."

"Not so jaded that I don't recognize a jewel when I see one," he said, looking straight at her.

She couldn't afford to take what he was saying to heart. Not tonight, their last night. They'd just finished dinner. Nathan's housekeeper had had the meal ready for them when they had arrived. After serving them, she'd left.

Dani gave the view another speculative glance. "Of course I'm not sure how you'd get out of here fast if you wanted to."

He grinned. "So what are you saying? That you want to get out of here fast?"

"Actually I was thinking of you."

"What about me?"

"Don't you ever wake up to a beautiful day and chafe to get outside as fast as you can?"

He chuckled. "I can assure you, that if I wanted to get out of here fast, there's more than one way I could."

She nodded. Of course he could. He was a Damaron, accustomed to things working his way, which was just one of the reasons why saying goodbye to him was going to be so hard.

He would fight her because he wasn't yet ready to let her go. Perhaps in another few weeks he would be, though that was just a guess since she had no idea how long his affairs usually lasted. But she couldn't afford to wait around and find out. Her heart was too involved already. "You have no garden here, do you?"

"You mean on the roof? No, that's the helipad. Remember?"

"I remember. I just wasn't certain I'd seen the entire roof."

He grinned. "You would have if you'd looked

down at any time during the takeoff or the landing."

Her lips twisted wryly. "That's something I tried very hard *not* to do."

With a chuckle, he framed her face with his hands and pressed a butterfly-light kiss to her lips that left her wanting more. "I did notice that. Something about your tightly closed eyes gave me my first clue. What were you afraid of? That you'd fall out of the helicopter if you looked down?"

She closed her hands over his thick wrists, smiled up at him, and nearly got lost in the depths of his dark gray eyes. "Let's just say I didn't want to take any chances."

"I wouldn't have let you fall."

"So you would have caught me?"

"Oh, yeah," he said, his eyes and voice softening. "Although I have to say I've never seen a single person fall out of one of our helicopters. You see," he said, his voice amused and kind, "Damaron helicopters are designed *not* to drop people."

She poked him lightly in the chest. "You're making fun of me, aren't you?"

"Why, I'm *shocked* that you'd even think of such a thing." All at once he frowned down at her. "You're not afraid of heights, are you? Because if you are, you should have told me—"

She started to nod, intending to tease him for a while, but then she decided she wouldn't be able to keep it up for any length of time, at least not with a straight face. "No, I'm not afraid of anything." Except getting to a point of no return with Nathan, where she wouldn't be able to leave him and would have to wait for him to leave her. That pain, she knew, would be intolerable. No, her plan was infinitely better.

Releasing her, he laughed and moved back to the table.

She loved his laugh, she thought as she watched him. It was husky and full-bodied, and it always gave her a sense of accomplishment when she heard it, because he was usually laughing at something she'd said or done. Tonight, his laughter mixed with music—a beautiful, lyrical, melody played by an orchestra flowed out from unseen speakers and filled the entire apartment.

She continued to watch him as he folded up his sleeves and started clearing off the table. "This is certainly a sight I didn't think I'd see."

"What's that?" he asked with a glance her way.

"You clearing the dishes. Who taught you to do that?"

"No one that I can remember."

In a way, she decided, it made sense that he wouldn't be able to stand leaving dirty dishes sitting out. He was the banker of the family, which meant he would be meticulous, even when it came to household chores. That trait also transferred to his lovemaking. Last night he'd left no spot on her body untouched or unkissed.

And tonight, just the thought of their passion had her body preparing itself in anticipation of the night of lovemaking to come. She could feel it in the new achiness of her breasts and the sudden throbbing between her legs. Before Nathan, she would have never believed her body could be so traitorous.

And the lovemaking *would* come. Nathan's intent was in his eyes every time he looked at her, it was in the feel of his mouth every time he paused to press a light kiss to her lips, it was in his touch whenever he brushed by her.

He scooped up the last of the dishes, then with his free hand and a napkin wiped down the portion of the long dining table they'd used. "I'll be back in a minute."

She gazed down the gleaming length of the table, at a tall pillar candle with eight burning wicks. All evening she'd managed to hold back her sadness, but each tick of the clock brought her that much closer to the time when she would be saying goodbye to Nathan for the final time.

As she'd told Cecilia, she knew only one way to deal with the sadness and the emotional pain she was feeling. Dance. For as long as she could remember, it had always been that way. Some things were simply too painful to hold inside. Such emotions had to come out some way. With her, the best way, the only way really, had always been to dance them out.

Before she could think about what she was doing, she kicked off her slippers, climbed up on the table, and began to move down its length in time to the music.

It would be so easy to just stay by Nathan's side for as long as he wanted her, go into his arms whenever he beckoned, make love with him whenever possible. But she couldn't.

She didn't know if it was possible for Nathan to love her. Regardless, her decision to leave him would have to be the same. Because even if he did fall in love with her, sooner or later he would ask for something she could not give. A family. And it would kill her not to be able to give him something he wanted so much.

Oh, sure, there was an alternative—adoption. And for herself, if she ever got to the point where she thought she'd be able to afford a child, she would love to adopt. And if Nathan truly loved her, he might even agree.

Except she couldn't even begin to calculate how hard it would be on a child to be raised in a family where every other child was born with a silver streak in their hair. From what she could tell, the silver streak not only marked one as unique, it made you a member of an extremely exclusive club that instantly, permanently bonded one member with another.

And if she stayed with Nathan without his love, then the day would come when he would say goodbye to her and she would be crushed beyond belief.

There was no way she could win. Leaving was her only recourse.

So she danced out her sorrow on the rhythmic currents of the music, the full skirt of her pink dress flaring to her upper thighs as she turned. Down the length of the table she went, then back, circling the burning wicks of the candle, in truth, dancing too close to the flames. Yet she continued because her heart felt as if it was breaking.

Time passed, the music changed, and still she danced. There was nothing precise or balletic about her steps. There were only emotion and graceful movement as she arched, swirled, and leaped up and down the table, her bare feet flying.

"Dani?"

She paused on her tiptoes and looked down at Nathan.

"Would you believe no one has ever danced on my table before?" he asked huskily.

She didn't know whether it had been the dancing or the sight of Nathan with the now familiar heated darkness in his eyes, but whatever it had been, her sadness was magically gone, leaving her filled with only love and desire.

And it had happened just in time, she realized. She'd almost made an awful mistake. She'd almost spent the entire evening brooding over the sadness that she knew would come tomorrow, when the reality was, she and Nathan had the whole night before them.

She slowly smiled at him. "You don't say."

He nodded. "I do say."

"That's hard for me to believe. It's such a perfect surface, but then I guess some people have no imagination."

"Apparently not."

"Then . . ." Another impulse hit her. Since this would be their last night together, she might as well go for broke. As a dancer, she had the ability to interpret music any way she chose, and in this case, she decided to change the rhythm and movement of her dance and make it more sensual and seductive.

With her hands on her waist at her back, she slinked her way across the table to him, her pelvis thrust toward him. Then just as he was about to reach up for her, she playfully retreated. Each successive time she advanced, her hip movements were more provocative, more tantalizing, and she came closer and closer to him. Yet each time he reached for her, his hands found only air.

She'd never in her life done such a thing, but she loved Nathan and he appeared to be absolutely poleaxed by her performance. She couldn't have asked for a better reaction from him, or a better audience. It gave her confidence to take her performance to an even more sensual level.

Entwining her arms above her head again and again, she danced in a serpentine manner around the candle, hitching her hips, first one way, then another, a combination of a Gypsy dance and a striptease. Then, in front of him once again, she slowly bent her knees and swiveled her hips from side to side.

"Dani . . ." Her name sounded strangled in his throat.

She twirled on her toes so that her back was to him. Then she reached for the top of the zipper of her pink dress and began to draw it down, inch by inch. And all the while her hips kept circling and undulating.

When the zipper arrived at the bottom, inches below her waist, she drew her arms from the dress's sleeveless top, then holding the loose fabric against her breasts, she turned and looked down at Nathan. For a moment she thought he'd stopped breathing. But then his breath came out in one large, shaky whoosh.

"You're killing me," he muttered thickly.

A thrill shot through her. "You look fine to me."

"I'll die if I don't have you now." He lifted his arms to her. "Come down."

She laughed. "Not yet."

She stepped back and released the dress. It fell to the table to puddle around her feet, leaving her clothed in only a lace bra and a narrow pair of panties. Nathan drew in a ragged breath. "Dani . . ."

"Not yet." She hooked a toe into the dress and, with a light kick sent it flying toward Nathan. He caught it with one hand, held it to his nose, and inhaled.

The raw need in his expression shook her. She began to tremble. She also began to doubt if she could continue the dance with the same calm, fun attitude with which she'd started. But she still had two scraps of lacy material to do away with and she was determined not to end her dance prematurely.

She heard the music change again, felt the throb of the bass line, and continued. Hooking her fingers in the elastic top of her panties, she slowly, enticingly, skimmed them down over her undulating hips and silken legs. Then, as before, she sent them flying in Nathan's direction. Except this time she deliberately flung it high over his head. Still he caught them, held them to his nose, and inhaled.

She almost stumbled.

Rotating her hips, she quickly finished the job by unclasping her bra and letting it drop to the table.

Nathan flung aside her dress and panties, then held out his arms to her. "Come down to me," he said, his voice sharp and demanding. Clearly he was a man who had reached his limit. He wasn't alone.

She leaned down and placed her hands on his shoulders. He caught her waist, lifted her against his body, and immediately began to kiss her. Her toes weren't even touching the floor, but she didn't care. All that mattered was this man, right now, and the way they made each other feel.

"I can't wait," he muttered, sitting her on the table. "Lie down."

Making love on the table made perfect sense, she thought through a red-hot haze. Neither of them could wait. Her heart beat with an almost unbearable excitement as she lay down and watched as he stripped out of his clothes.

"Hurry," she murmured. "Oh God, hurry."

Her arms reached for him, her legs spread. He positioned himself on top of her and thrust deeply into her.

A fiery shock of pleasure jolted through her, then another and another. There was no time, no place, or even discomfort from the hard table. There was only Nathan, her, and an inferno that raged inside her.

He held great power over her. He made her want, need, desire. He had set the fire to blazing inside her and he was the only man in the world who could put out the flames.

She drove her fingers up into his hair, her tongue into his mouth. She held on to him as tightly as she could and whispered words of longing and hunger.

His hips moved in a fast, primitive rhythm. A helpless sound escaped her lips as her breasts swelled and ached. Heat coiled in her belly, pooled in her lower limbs, took over her mind.

There was nothing delicate or sweet about this lovemaking. It was raw and primitive and everything she needed. Time after time her hips jerked upward to meet his. Time after time she thought she'd surely burst from the sheer heat of the experience. And then it started . . . the spasms of her climax that gripped her with ecstasy, madness, and finally, *finally*, sweet release.

She was in a bed, she thought hazily. She could feel the softness of the covers beneath her, Nathan's warm body against her side, his heavy arm across her waist.

She had a vague memory of his lifting her into his arms after their lovemaking and carrying her off, but that was where her memory failed her. Obviously she'd dozed off somewhere between the dining room and his bedroom. She did remember how strong his arms had been around her, though, and how sated and exhausted her own body had felt.

She eased over on her side so that she was facing him. His eyes opened.

"Sorry," she murmured. "I didn't mean to wake you."

A slight smile touched his lips. "Why not?"

She giggled and couldn't believe that she had. The last time she'd giggled she'd been nine years old. "Well, because, I thought you might need to sleep. Sooner or later most human beings need to."

"Not me. Not when I've got you in bed with me. Besides, we did manage to get a couple of hours of sleep."

"We did?"

"Uh-huh."

He lifted a hand to brush her hair back from her face. It was the first time she realized her hair had come unbraided. Where was the pink rose? she wondered.

"Do you know what time it is?"

He shook his head. "All I can say for sure is that

it's still dark outside, which means it's not daylight yet."

"Brilliant deduction."

"Thank you."

She traced the silver streak in his hair, then she realized what she was doing and stopped. Somehow, and from this point onward, she needed to keep a clear head. "Okay, just for my own benefit, where would I find a clock if I wanted to pin down the time a little better?"

He pulled her against him and she felt the hard length of his arousal pressed against her stomach. "My watch is on the night table on my side of the bed."

"Oh, good," she said a bit breathlessly. "The same side you're facing away from." She paused while he pressed a kiss to her neck. "I don't suppose I could talk you into turning over and checking it for me, could I?"

Solemnly he shook his head, then kissed a different place on her neck. "I have no interest in the time."

Ordinarily she might not either. Except for tonight, their last night together. She had a fervent need to see how many more hours she would have with him. Or wouldn't have. Masochistic, she supposed, but she couldn't help herself. She had to plan what she would say to him very carefully.

"The only thing that really interests me right now is keeping you just where you are for as long as I can," he said, his voice husky.

With his rigid sex pressed against her, Dani was all too aware of her own body softening and heating once again, readying itself for more lovemaking. And she was torn. She wanted to make love to him one final time almost more than she wanted to draw her next breath. But that would be self-defeating.

She had to give herself enough time to convince Nathan that it would be best if they didn't see each other again. She also had to come up with a *way* to do it, something she hadn't been able to do as yet.

The truth was, she didn't have a clue how to go about it. Her body betrayed her every time he looked at her, much less kissed her, and tonight had been a prime example of that. Her impulsiveness had led her into that impromptu striptease, when her cause would have been better served if she'd simply sat him down after dinner and presented him with a logical reason why they should part. Except logic didn't have a thing to do with all that had happened between Nathan and her since they'd met.

And lying in his arms wasn't helping her situation one bit.

Deliberately quick, she pushed away from him, slipped from the bed, and grabbed up the first thing she saw to cover herself, the comforter from the top of the bed.

Nathan sat up. "What do you think you're doing?"

"I told you. I wanted to see what time it was."

"Hell, Dani, if I'd known you were that serious, I would have—"

"Never mind. I found a clock." She lifted on her tiptoes to read the small gold clock atop his bureau. "It's a little after four." Her heart sank at how late it was. Dawn would be breaking in a couple of hours.

"Okay. You found out what time it is. *Now* would you come back to bed?" He pulled back the covers and looked pointedly at the empty space beside him.

She did her best to ignore him. Instead, she chose to pace back and forth in front of the bed, the hem of the comforter trailing after her like a train. "I was just wondering. . . ."

"Can't you wonder in bed?"

Despite the fact that his voice was hard and nowhere near a plea, she couldn't help but give a rueful chuckle. "No, actually I don't seem to think very well in bed."

He plumped a few pillows behind him, then leaned back against them. "A bed is not meant for thinking, Dani."

"Uh-huh. I know." She pulled the comforter tighter against her.

He loudly sighed. "Okay. What are you wondering?"

"I was wondering where we are in our game."

"Game?"

She nodded. "You know—the game of who owes who. Let's see. This afternoon you owed me because Helene went ahead and wrote you the check, then you paid that off by giving me dinner. And then—"

"And then you did the sexiest striptease I've ever seen, so I think that means I owe you."

"No." She shook her head. "Then we had sex and I think that negated everything."

He stirred restlessly. "I think we should leave sex out of our game. I please you. You please me. When it comes to sex, we're perfectly matched, which means we're even. Come back to bed and I'll demonstrate."

"I, uh, agree with you that sex shouldn't be factored into the game. As you said, we're even. And actually, we're also even on everything else too. We should just let it go at that."

"Okay, that's fine by me. *Now* come back to bed."

She stopped pacing and turned to look at him. "There's something else, something more I need to tell you."

A wry grin twisted his lips. "Boy, do you ever know how to ruin the last couple of hours of a night."

"Sorry."

"Don't be, but at least come sit beside me while we talk. I also have something I need to tell you."

She hesitated, but in the end the pleasure she knew she would receive from simply being near him overruled her caution. She sat down beside him on the edge of the bed, still holding the comforter around her.

"Let me go first," he said, reaching for her free hand.

She nodded her consent and called herself ten kinds of coward for wanting to put off what she had to say, even for only a few minutes. But the truth was, she still wasn't sure how to approach what she needed to say. She did feel her first step had gone well, though. By telling him they were even in their game, she'd taken away the possibility that he might say they needed to continue to see each other because one of them still owed the other. "What is it?"

"Tomorrow. Today . . . This afternoon, actually. I have to return to Europe and I'll be there for three weeks."

The surprise instinctively had her pulling her hand away, but in this case, he anticipated what she would do and tightened his hold on her hand.

"I want you to know, Dani, that I haven't deliberately kept this news from you. The trip has been on my agenda for quite some time, but when you and I met, the trip got pushed to the back of my mind."

"I see." He was leaving anyway, she thought sadly. Even if she had put off her decision to part from him, it wouldn't have done her any good. And his trip might actually help her. If she knew they were separated geographically, she wouldn't be tempted to pick up the phone and call him, or to go see him. "You were certainly under no obligation to tell me anything about your schedule, Nathan. I'd have to be an idiot not to know that you're a busy man."

"Dani, don't. Stop."

"What?"

"I'm not sure, but I have this feeling you're withdrawing from me."

An astute observation, she reflected. "No, really, I do understand, Nathan. I understand completely."

He eyed her carefully. "Good. Then I hope you'll be equally understanding about what I'm going to say next. Dani, I want you to come with me."

There went her reprieve from temptation. She shook her head. "There's no way I can do that."

"Don't say no immediately. Think about it."

"I don't have to. I can't go. I have classes to give and a spring recital to choreograph."

"I'm talking about three weeks in Europe, Dani. Think of the fun we could have together."

"Fun? You'll be there to conduct business, right? Where would the fun come into it?"

"I won't be working twenty-four hours a day. And once we get over there, I'll make sure we have a lot of time to sightsee and shop." He lifted her hand and pressed a kiss to the sensitive skin of her palm. A shiver of heat ran down her spine. "And then there'll be the hours we can spend in bed together."

She shook her head again as if to add emphasis to her refusal. "I can't afford to be gone three weeks."

"Are you talking about being unable to afford the trip *financially*, or in some other way?"

"In every way." She tore her hand from his and stood. "Teaching ballet may not seem like a very important occupation to you—"

"*Don't* put words in my mouth, Dani. I've never said that, nor have I ever thought it."

"My students depend on me. There's not only my regular students to think about, but now there's also Cecilia. She's going to start day after tomorrow." She threw a glance at him over her shoulder and wished like hell she wasn't so tempted to go with him. He kept telling her to think about it, but the reality was, she didn't have to think more than a second to know that three weeks alone with him in Europe would be glorious. In fact, three weeks alone with him *anywhere* would be glorious. And afterward she would have memories that would last for the rest of her life.

"Dani?"

What would three more weeks with him hurt? she asked herself. And the extra heated hours she would be able to spend in his arms . . . And if she was going to feel hurt anyway, did it really make any difference whether it was tonight or three weeks from now?

Stop!

The word shrilled so loudly in her head, she was afraid she'd shouted it. She glanced at him, but his expression hadn't changed. He hadn't heard. Mentally she made an effort to pull herself together.

Unfortunately, she'd been over her decision too many times. She knew exactly what and whom it would hurt. *Her.*

"Dani?"

"I can't do it, Nathan. I simply can't do it. And not only for the reasons I just gave you."

"There's more?"

Again she began to pace along the foot of the bed. "You remember I said that I had something to tell you?"

He followed her progress back and forth across the floor with his hard gaze. "I remember."

"Well, it's just this. You and I . . . we happened much too fast. I'm overwhelmed. If you'll remember, I tried to tell you something like this before we made love for the first time."

"I remember. I also remember I discounted it. Nothing you do or say makes me believe that I overwhelm you."

"You're talking about your viewpoint. I'm trying to tell you my viewpoint. Look, I know that I was the one who started everything between us that night in Paris, but it was just a game. I never intended things to go this far." She nodded toward the bed. "I'm not accustomed to such a grand and fast lifestyle."

He muttered a highly volatile epithet. "That's ridiculous and you know it."

She did, but that was beside the point. "And there's more. While I enjoy being with you—"

"I would say you did a bit more than *enjoy* this evening, wouldn't you?" He drawled the words out.

She was losing her argument, because, heaven help her, she agreed with everything he was saying. It was time to pull out all the stops. "The truth is, Nathan, I can't see any point in continuing our relationship."

"Then you're very shortsighted."

If the icy edge in his voice had been a knife, it would have cut her. "The sex is great, there's no doubt about it, but we've done that now, and well"—she shrugged—"as far as I can see, there's not too much else going on between us."

Stark naked, he sprang from the bed, his face like thunder. "I see. So we don't have enough to talk about? We don't have fun together? We're not compatible? Is that what you're saying, Dani? Because if that's what you're saying, then you're lying."

She turned to face him. "Sometimes everything can be right, Nathan, and still be wrong."

"That makes absolutely zero sense, Dani. *Zero.*"

"Maybe not, but it's the case here."

"And what about what happened between us tonight? On the table. On the bed."

"It was sex, Nathan. Just more sex. Don't you get it? I'm just not interested in seeing you anymore. Accept it. Deal with it. Go to Europe and have a nice three weeks. But when you get back, don't call me, because I plan to get on with my life."

His face had gone even darker, a vein pulsed in his forehead. Truthfully, he looked as if he were about to kill her. It took everything that was in her to force a smile to her face. "It's been fun and interesting, Nathan. Have a great rest of your life."

EIGHT

Nathan Damaron wasn't a man to accept no for an answer, nor was he a man who gave up if he wanted something badly enough.

She should have known that about him, Dani reflected, and she supposed she might have if she'd stopped to give the matter any thought. But she'd been too caught up in the pain of having to break it off with him to consider how he might react.

She'd guessed he might be angry. After all, powerful men weren't accustomed to having their wishes thwarted. Still, she'd been shocked at the ferocity of his anger. He hadn't raised his voice, nor had he threatened her in any way, but when she'd left his apartment that morning, she'd had the sure feeling she'd narrowly escaped danger.

Not that she believed he would have physically hurt her. But she'd sensed an unfamiliar type of violence simmering just below his surface.

That had been almost two weeks ago. Since then, he'd called her daily, usually more than once. He'd also sent one exquisite flower arrangement after the other, so many in fact, she'd started giving them out to her neighbors in the brownstones on either side of her.

But it was the calls that were the hardest for her to handle. Each time she had to endure arguing with him all over again. It was getting more and more impossible for her, because she was not only having to battle him, but herself as well. As a result, she'd had to start using her answering machine to screen her calls.

Since he'd been gone, the days had been interminable for her and the nights had been even longer. It took a real effort for her to get through either. She kept telling herself that each new day would be better, but so far no such luck.

She recognized that she was in mourning, that once again she'd lost someone she loved. But oddly enough, the fact that Nathan wasn't dead made it worse on her. Gil's death had been a fact she couldn't change. She'd had no alternative but to let him go.

But this time she knew Nathan still wanted her, and because he did, she knew she could have him for a little while longer. She could, that is, if only she were braver.

But she wasn't. The pain she'd felt when Gil had died, along with the surrounding complexities of the accident, had nearly done her in. By breaking off with Nathan now, she was doing her best to ensure she never felt that much pain again.

Unfortunately, her plan wasn't working so far.

Dani's gaze swept over her afternoon class of ladies. Some were housewives, others were doctors, one was a lawyer, and two of them were former professional dancers. All, though, had one thing in common. Their love of ballet.

Today, however, their minds didn't seem to be with her. Maybe it was the beautiful weather they were having outside. Even she was having trouble today, which was unusual for her. Normally she attacked the barre and was a stickler for perfection in herself and in her students. But today, she found herself in sympathy and her tone was mild as she chastised them.

"Ladies, ladies, you're not concentrating. Instead of getting shorter, you're supposed to be getting taller. And your leg positions—they're all over the place."

Her students laughed good-naturedly as Dani walked over to the record player, lifted the needle, then set it down. The same music began to play again.

Back at the barre once more, Dani took up her position. "*Piqués* with *dégagé, plié, relevé.* Pay attention—inside, outside, *relevé.* Hold. Now turn into the barre, wait for the music, and begin again."

When the exercise was completed for the other

leg, she stopped the music. "Good. That was better. This time we are going to do *grands ronds de jambe* and let's do eight. Finish in front on the eighth, open-arm *allongé*. Bend forward from the waist and raise the leg and arm together. Got it?" Groans resounded throughout the studio. She smiled. "I just know you are all going to love this. Okay, let's go." The record player needle was reset once more and music swelled out into the studio. "Colleen, don't kick from the knee, *stretch* from the knee. The quickest way to ruin that kneecap is to kick."

Nathan watched Dani from the hall, his position angled so that unless she knew exactly where to look, she wouldn't see him. As for him, he couldn't take his eyes off her. She was wearing a pink low-backed leotard with pink tights and a pink sheer skirt tied around her waist. Ragged black leg warmers went from her ankle to up over her knee. Pink satin slippers finished off her ensemble. And her hair. It was done up in that witchy way she'd worn it when they'd gone to Helene's.

He'd spent enough nights at the ballet, watching the greats of the ballet world, to recognize that she was extremely talented. She'd said it had been her decision after the accident to teach, but it must have been a hard decision for her. And of course, her career wasn't all she'd lost because of the accident. She'd lost the boy she'd loved.

A now familiar pang of jealousy wrenched through him. He knew the boy was dead, but that boy had had Dani's heart for however long the two of them had been together. In contrast, he'd always had the feeling Dani was withholding a part of herself from him. Not when they made love—but the rest of the time.

Then again, since when did he need a woman's heart to be happy? He didn't, he assured himself. All he wanted was to keep Dani in his life until he decided he didn't want her there anymore.

Europe had been hell without her there by his side. It was why he'd come straight from the airport today to see her. He'd been starved for the sight of her.

That last night they'd spent together, as well as the countless times he'd talked to her on the phone while he'd been in Europe, she'd said everything a woman could say to a man to get him to accept her decision to break up. Yet he couldn't accept her words, just as he couldn't stop himself from coming to see her today.

Standing in the hallway, he took in everything about her—the humor in her voice as she gave directions to the women, the exquisiteness of her every movement and position, the obvious power of her slight body and its incredible flexibility. Lord help him, it made him remember the hot, steamy hours they'd spent together making love.

Dani clapped her hands together, bringing Nathan out of his reverie. "Stretch period. Those of you who haven't already done so, put on your toe shoes."

He moved to the center of the doorway, waiting for her to catch sight of him.

Smiling over a comment from one of her students, Dani turned and lifted her head. That's when she saw him. The smile faded, her body stiffened, and her face paled.

"Nathan." Her lips moved to form his name, though he couldn't be sure she'd actually spoken his name aloud.

For a moment she simply stared at him without moving. Then, around her, her class slowly went quiet, as one by one the women caught sight of him. Quickly she walked to him.

"Please step out into the hall, Nathan." Her voice was low with a slight tremor. "I'm in the middle of a class."

He moved away from the door. "I can see that and I won't bother you long. I'm just here to ask if you'll have dinner with me this evening."

She closed the door to her studio. "No. What are you even doing back here anyway? Wasn't your trip supposed to last through next week?"

"Yes, but I cut the trip short. I needed to see you."

"You came back because of *me*?"

She looked so amazed, he almost laughed. "You find that hard to believe?"

"Actually I do. I can't imagine a Damaron allowing a woman to interfere with his work."

"There was no *allowing* about it. I couldn't sit in a meeting, go out to dinner, fall asleep at night, wake up in the morning, or even pick up a pencil, without my mind wandering to you, wondering what you were doing and if you were with someone else."

She looked down at her slippers. "I'm sorry."

"You damn well should be."

Her head came up and fire flashed in her eyes. "Why? Because I had the temerity to stand up to you and say no?"

"Because you haven't been able to explain to my satisfaction why you broke it off with me."

She threw out her hands. "That's not my problem, Nathan, nor is it my responsibility. I've said everything I can on the subject. The rest is up to you."

"I don't believe you."

Instantly her brows drew together. "What? What don't you believe?"

"I don't believe you've said everything you can. There has to be something more to all of this."

Her arms slipped around her waist. "That's insane, Nathan."

"Maybe. Maybe not."

"Why would you think I would hold back anything from you?"

"Because what you've said so far makes no sense to me."

"Which puts us right back where we started. Nathan, your inability to make sense of it is not my problem." She sighed heavily. "Look, normally I'm sure you're the one who walks away in your relationships and this . . . this situation must be very different for you. But if you look at it logically and realize that you and I have known each other such a short time, it makes a lot of sense."

She glanced over her shoulder at her students in the studio, then at her watch. "I've got to get back to the class." She looked up at him. "You'll be all right, Nathan. Just because I didn't think it was right between us doesn't mean your next girl will think that."

As she turned to go he grabbed her wrist. "Dammit, Dani. I don't need analyzing, nor do I need consoling."

She stared up at him for what seemed like minutes, but what must have been only moments. "Okay, you're right. There is something else I haven't told you, because I knew it would hurt you."

"Hurt me more than you already have, you mean?"

She flinched. "John," she said. "It's John. He and I—"

Something stabbed him near his heart. "You told me you were only friends." He released her.

"We are. But all along there's been something else between us. And now—"

"You're lovers? Is that what you're trying to tell me?"

She looked stricken. "I—"

"How long? Never mind, I don't want to know."

"I'm sorry," she whispered, shaking her head.

"I'm really sorry." Then she hurried back into her studio and shut the door quietly behind her.

He rubbed his fingers across his forehead, feeling as if he'd just been run over by a steamroller, and at the same time feeling as if something had put a huge hole in him.

Almost blind with anger and hopelessness, he stomped out of the building and flung himself into the back of his limo. With a gesture of his hand to his driver, he started the car toward the Damaron Tower.

Staring sightlessly out the window, he brooded over everything that had happened since Dani had kissed him on the Paris quay that night, and he tried to make new sense out of it.

Dani was right when she'd said they'd known each other such a short time. With them, it had been fast and hot. But what was so wrong with that?

The sex they'd had that last night they'd been together had been fantastic, but she'd shrugged it off by saying she needed more than sex. More? He didn't have a clue what she was talking about. As far as he was concerned, he'd enjoyed every minute he'd spent with her, both in and *out* of bed. And he would have bet a fortune that she had too.

But during the last two weeks she'd continued to say she didn't want to see him again, and now she'd finally told him why. *John.*

Now everything made sense, and he'd be crazy to continue pursuing her. *Crazy.* What he really wanted to do was kill John, then kidnap Dani, and keep her with him until she forgot the other man. But that would be even crazier.

He scrubbed his eyes. He was tired, he realized. He'd just pushed three weeks of meetings into less than two, then hurried home to find that Dani and John were lovers.

He leaned his head back and closed his eyes. Dani had been right when she'd said that he was the one who'd always ended relationships. Was that why he'd been so unwilling to let her go, and was still unwilling even now that he knew she loved John?

No. Injured pride would not be enough to have drilled this hole in his stomach and filled it with the fiery pain of knowing he might never know another day of her smiles, or another night of her fire.

Maybe he just needed to give himself time. Time to rest. Maybe even time to date other women.

It wasn't conceit on his part to believe there were literally dozens of women far more beautiful than Dani who would love the opportunity to go out with him. He knew it for a fact and had known it ever since he'd turned fifteen. His name and money ensured it.

But Dani hadn't even known who he was when she'd kissed him on the quay. Hadn't known even as she was melting in his arms . . .

Hell. He'd never needed any one particular woman in his life, and he sure as hell didn't need Dani.

—◈———————◈—

With one hand holding a casserole and the other hand holding the door open, John bent to view Dani's refrigerator. "What's going on, Dani?"

"What do you mean?" Dani asked from her perch atop her kitchen counter.

"In your refrigerator." John used his body to prop open the door as he tried to rearrange the contents.

"Oh, well, let's see. There's a lightbulb in there the manufacturer *says* goes off when you close the door, though I'm not sure I believe them. And then there's a motor that keeps everything cold, though I couldn't tell you where it is. Why? Are the vegetables fraternizing in an unseemly manner?"

John finally shoved the casserole into a space he'd freed up, straightened, and closed the door. He fixed a stern gaze on her. "You're not living up to your part of our bargain."

Her mind wandering as it so often did these days, she twisted a strand of hair around a finger, then unwound it again.

"Dani?"

She looked back at John. "What? Oh, the . . . um . . . bargain. What bargain would that be?"

"The bargain where I cook and you eat."

"Oh, *that* bargain." She nodded. "Right."

With a frown, he leaned against an opposite counter. "What's up, Dani? You haven't seemed yourself for days now."

She shrugged. "Nothing's up as far as I know. I just haven't been particularly hungry these days." Food simply hadn't appealed to her lately, but then nothing else had either. She'd been conducting her ballet classes by rote, which wasn't like her at all.

He shook his head, his expression troubled. "I haven't said anything up to now, but I'm worried about you."

She looked at him in surprise. "Don't be. I'm fine."

"I'm not so sure. You've always weighed practically nothing anyway, but now I think you're actually losing weight. You're not becoming anorexic on me, are you?"

She leveled a rueful gaze on him. "Please tell me you don't really believe that. I mean, really, John. You know me better than that."

He appeared unmoved. "Dani, your bones are sticking out."

"You're exaggerating."

"Have you *looked* at yourself in a mirror lately?"

"How can I help it when an entire wall of my studio is mirrored?" She slipped off the counter and went to pour herself a glass of water, all the while wondering if she really had looked at herself in the mirror lately. She watched her students, but she couldn't remember checking her own positions lately.

"Dani, there's something wrong with you, something odd, and you can't convince me otherwise."

Nathan. He was what was wrong with her, she

reflected. He'd taken over her body and mind. Even though it had been three weeks since that afternoon when he'd returned from Europe and she'd led him to believe she was in love with John—something John didn't know—Nathan had continued to be in her every waking thought and in her every sleeping dream. Some nights she woke up, her body aching, covered in sweat, convinced that if she looked over, she'd see him there.

"You do realize you're not yourself, don't you?"

She smiled gently. "Yes, I do, and let me reassure you. There's absolutely nothing wrong with me except an old-fashioned case of lovesickness."

"Nathan?"

She nodded. There, she thought. She hadn't even wanted to admit it to herself, but after five weeks without Nathan she'd had to face the fact that she might never be cured of him. She wasn't being dramatic or even premature about her judgment. She just knew. The knowledge was a blazing pain in her bones, in her heart, and in every fiber of her being.

However, she had no doubt he was cured of her. In the last three weeks he hadn't tried to see her or call her, and as each agonizingly long day had passed she'd finally realized that she'd been successful in convincing him that the two of them would never work.

If she'd needed further proof that he had gone on with his life, she'd gotten it several times over when she opened the society page on four different occasions and seen a picture of him at some affair or other with a beautiful woman draped by his side, a *different* woman each time.

She'd done everything she could think of to get Nathan to forget her and had finally succeeded by lying to him about John. Now he'd forgotten about her. How ironic, since she was finding it impossible to forget him.

John narrowed his eyes on her. "Maybe it is Nathan and maybe it isn't. And maybe Nathan is only part of it. I don't know. But if this malaise of yours continues, and you don't go to see a doctor, I'm going to pick you up and carry you to a doctor myself."

"Okay, girls. We're going to start off with our *demi-pliés* in the first, second, fourth, and fifth positions. Then we'll move on to the *grand pliés* and the *port à bras*, six times each."

She set the record to play then moved quickly to the barre. She did each movement with the four girls, all the time watching them carefully. "Stacy, that position is *not* in ballet. Pay attention. Cecilia, where's your center? Remember, everything is centered from the diaphragm."

Cecilia giggled and obediently tried again.

"Better," she responded with a smile.

The four girls made up one of her private classes and she'd fought Helene to put Cecilia in it. Helene had wanted a one-on-one class for Cecilia, but Dani had finally been able to convince Helene that her granddaughter would gain greater benefit from being in a class with girls her own age.

"Marcia, what on earth is wrong with you? Your legs look like wet noodles." All four girls giggled.

Still, she'd taken a gamble by putting Cecilia into this class and she was relieved and glad to say the young girl was flourishing. It had taken Cecilia just one class to become friends with the three girls, and even the fact that she'd forgotten certain things and was more awkward than the others didn't seem to upset her. And it was helpful that the other three girls had instinctively become both protectors and cheerleaders for Cecilia. Helene was overjoyed.

A wave of nausea and dizziness hit Dani. Her grip on the barre tightened suddenly and she felt her balance giving way. Before she knew what was happening, she dropped to the floor in a sitting position.

All four girls ran to her in alarm. "What's wrong, Miss Savourat?"

"Are you all right?"

"Yes, yes, I'm fine." She held a hand to her forehead. This had happened to her twice in the last week or so, but not with this severity. Maybe John was right. Maybe she should go see a doctor.

"I'll go get you a glass of water," Elizabeth said, then ran off to do it.

"What happened?" Cecilia asked.

"I—" Dani's hand flew to her mouth as the nausea rose in her throat.

"It's all right, Cecilia." Stacy nodded knowingly

at Dani. "You feel like you're going to throw up, don't you?"

She was having to concentrate on *not* throwing up and couldn't answer her.

"And you were dizzy, weren't you?" Stacy went on. "I know all about that. That's how my mom feels every time she gets pregnant."

Pregnant. The nausea began to subside and Dani waited several beats, then cautiously took her hand away from her mouth. "I am not pregnant, Stacy. I think it's just a little hot in here."

Elizabeth raced back to her and handed her a glass of water. Gratefully she took it and sipped. She supposed her symptoms did replicate those of early pregnancy, but in her case, it wasn't true. It couldn't be true.

"Are you *sure* you're not pregnant?" Stacy persisted.

"Yes." A cold, sick feeling suddenly gripped her and slowly she turned her head and looked in the mirror. A pale face stared back at her. Her gaze dropped lower to her breasts and stayed. Was she imagining it or were they slightly larger? No, she had to be imagining it. She'd always had small breasts and like most dancers she took her body for granted, never giving it a second thought. But now . . .

She stood. "Elizabeth, thank you for the water. Okay, girls, back to the barre."

"Nathan. *Nathan.*"

With a start, he refocused on the beautiful blonde sitting beside him. "I'm sorry. Were you saying something, Jessica?"

He was bored, but he hadn't realized he'd tuned her out so completely.

She laughed. "As a matter of fact I was. Why weren't you listening to me?" She stuck out her bottom lip in what, he was sure, she thought of as an irresistible pout.

Thinking fast, he reached into his jacket pocket and pulled out a leather-covered notepad with a gold pen and jotted down several random numbers. "I just had a thought about a business deal I've been working on." Jessica viewed business in a favorable light, he thought cynically, because she knew that without it, he would have no money.

"Business? Well, okay, as long as it's business, I'll forgive you. But you *must* hear this story of my Christmas vacation in Switzerland, because you're simply not going to believe what happened."

Out of the corner of his eyes, Nathan spotted a photographer who worked for one of New York's society columns, though off the top of his head he couldn't have said which one. Giving Jessica a winning smile, he reached for her hand and brought it to his lips just as the cameraman snapped off several shots. "Thank you for forgiving me, and if you wouldn't mind starting over again, I'd love to hear all about it."

Jessica beamed. "Well, first of all, there were a lot of our mutual friends there."

"Oh, really? Who?"

"For starters, Caroline and Bud Philips, Marion Colefax with William Masse, Lili Parr, and . . ."

The photographer made his way past them and Nathan tuned Jessica out again. As unobtrusively as possible he glanced at his watch, trying to figure out when he could gracefully suggest they leave. Unfortunately, he knew that Jessica wasn't going to want to leave unless she thought he would spend the night with her. But it wasn't going to happen.

When the night had begun, that had been his intention, his hope. He'd grown sick of the sleepless nights he'd been spending in his apartment. When he was there alone in the deep of the night, wandering through the rooms, praying for the unfeeling, unseeing, bliss of sleep to come, his mind would conjure up a vision of Dani as she'd been that last night she'd spent there, dancing up and down his dining-room table. And as she'd been in his bed, naked and sweet, her legs tangled with his, her misty blue eyes full of passion. One night he'd even thought he heard her laughter, ringing down the hallway.

Dani was haunting him. He'd had to get out of the apartment.

Several years ago, and for a relatively short period of time, he and Jessica had dated. She'd been fun, but he'd soon grown bored and called it off. Jessica, however, had never made any secret of the fact that she'd love to become Mrs. Nathan Damaron.

Normally he wouldn't have attended this dinner dance. Instead, he would have instructed his accountant to write out a check for the charity. But tonight he'd craved a woman's companionship—a woman who could make him smile and laugh, and at the same time make him want her. And so he had called Jessica.

It wasn't her fault that she could neither make him laugh nor make him want her.

"So there we were, waiting for the gondola and . . ."

His heart missed a beat as he caught sight of a woman on the dance floor with long, light brown hair, wearing a chiffon dress in the colors of the sea. She could be . . . But no, she wasn't. Of course she wasn't. Dani was probably at this very moment lying in John's arms on their roof-garden bed.

"Where's Dani?"

He barely kept from starting at the loud, foghornlike voice and glanced up at Helene Sorge, an extremely displeased expression creasing her face. He stood and forced a smile. "Hello, Helene. What a nice surprise."

"You didn't answer my question, Damaron. Where's Dani?"

"I'm afraid I don't know. Have you met my date, Jessica McNatton? Jessica, this is Helene Sorge."

"How do you do," Jessica said politely.

Helene barely glanced at her. "Why aren't you with Dani tonight?"

"Excuse me, but who's Dani?" Jessica asked.

"Damaron, if I find out you've hurt that little thing, I'll—"

"Helene," he said sharply, cutting her off before she could say anything more. "If you'll excuse us, we were just about to dance." He reached for Jessica's hand and drew her to her feet.

Helene's eyes narrowed on him. "Has Dani told you what a miracle she's accomplished with Cecilia?"

"I'm sincerely happy to hear it, and with the help of your extremely generous contribution this year, our new wing of the hospital will be able to help many more children like Cecilia."

He didn't wait for a response, but rather pulled Jessica onto the dance floor and within moments had them lost in the throng of the other dancers.

Jessica skillfully molded her body to his and wrapped her arm tightly around his neck, but instead of exciting him, it only served to remind him of the way Dani had flowed into his body the night they had danced, relaxed and natural, as if she had been made just for him.

Jessica smiled up at him. "I suppose you had to be polite to her because of the contribution you mentioned, but goodness, what a rude woman."

He couldn't summon any response. The vision in his mind had already switched to that of Dani as she'd been that afternoon in Connecticut—a pink rose in her hair, her dress spread around her as she sat on the grass with Cecilia, giving the child her entire attention.

"Nathan, you didn't answer me before. Who is this Dani person?"

"Oh, she's a woman who is helping Helene's granddaughter."

"That woman made this Dani sound as if she was a part of your life. Is she?"

"No."

He wasn't surprised to hear that Cecilia was doing well. Dani would be able to make a dead plant flourish with her warmth, her sense of fun, her caring. During the time he'd spent with her, he realized with something like surprise, he had actually felt as if *he* were flourishing.

Damnit all to hell.

He stopped dancing. "I'm not feeling well, Jessica. If you don't mind, I'll send you home in my car and I'll catch a cab."

"Don't be silly. You know that won't work. The driver of your car is your security guard for the night. He'd never allow you to go home in a cab."

He put a hand to his head, where to his astonishment he actually felt the beginnings of a real headache. "Then I'll put you in a cab. Come on."

She was silent until they reached the lobby of the hotel and then she pulled him to a halt in a fairly quiet area. "I'm not going to allow you to go home alone, Nathan. Not when you're feeling so badly. I can take care of you." Her expression turned coy. "I can make you feel better, or have you forgotten?"

"No, of course I haven't forgotten." He gestured to a bellman, and when the young man arrived, he handed him two fifty-dollar bills. "Please call Miss McNatton a cab and escort her into it. The first bill is for you. The second is for the cab."

"Yes, sir!" The young man looked at Jessica expectantly. "Right this way, Miss McNatton."

"But, Nathan, I—"

"Please, Jessica. I just need to get a good night's sleep. I'll feel much better in the morning."

"Then will you call me tomorrow?"

He hesitated, weighing his answer. Then he sighed. "No, Jessica, I'm sorry, but I won't." He lifted her hand and kissed it. "Thank you for a lovely evening. We will be seeing each other again at various functions, and I hope I can count on you as a friend."

"Bastard," she said softly, then slowly smiled. "Friend." She rose on her tiptoes and kissed his cheek. "If you ever need anything . . ."

"I'll call."

"Right," she said dryly. "Somehow I don't think I'll wait by the phone. Good-bye, Nathan."

"Good-bye, Jessica." He stood where he was and watched her until she disappeared through the hotel's doors, then withdrew his cell phone from his jacket pocket and punched in a number. "I'm ready to leave."

Jessica had asked if Dani were a part of his life

and he'd answered truthfully. No, she was not. No. No. *No.*

So why then did visions of her constantly cloud his mind? And why did his blood still run hot when he remembered their lovemaking? And why the hell couldn't he simply forget her?

Dani stared at the familiar still-life painting on the wall of Dr. Robison's examining room number 2. She'd seen the painting many times, just as she'd seen the other still lifes that were hanging in the other examining rooms. She even knew they had been painted by Dr. Robison's mother.

Dr. Robison had been the doctor who had cared for her after the accident. He had also been the one who had told her she would never bear children.

The door opened and the tall, silver-haired doctor walked in, her chart in his hand. He dropped down on a stool, opened her chart, and looked at her. "Dani, I don't know exactly how to tell you this, but, well, congratulations. You're pregnant."

"I'm—I'm . . . ? No." Darkness appeared at the edges of her vision. She shook her head. "You told me getting pregnant would be impossible. That my body had sustained too much damage . . ."

"I know that's what I said, and it was a sound diagnosis." He shook his head, his expression amazed. "But every once in a while in my business—not often enough, mind you, but every once in a while—a bona fide miracle happens, and it appears that that's what has happened to you." He smiled at her. "This is great news, Dani. I know how terribly unhappy you've been, knowing you could never have children of your own."

The darkness steadily advanced, threatening to close a curtain on her vision. She fought it. "But I— I don't understand. There must be some mistake."

Dr. Robison shook his head. "There's no mistake. I double-checked everything. It's time to celebrate, my dear. But"—he raised a finger—"you can't celebrate too much. You must take good care of yourself during this time. In fact, during these first few months of your pregnancy, I want you to modify your usual behavior so that you exert yourself as little as possible."

He reached for his prescription pad and began writing. "Don't stand when you can sit. Don't sit when you can lie down. And absolutely no dancing." He glanced at her over his reading glasses. "I'm not going to kid you, Dani. The damage to your body is still there, which means you may very well have trouble with this pregnancy. But I have no doubt that if you take extra-good care of yourself, you will be able to carry this baby to full term." He tore a prescription sheet off the pad and handed it to her. "This is for a prenatal vitamin that you need to start on immediately, and I want to see you back here in . . ."

The darkness closed in on her, and for the first time in her life, Dani fainted.

NINE

She was pregnant.

Dani lifted her arm and laid it above her head as she rested on the roof bed beneath the shade of the awning. Earlier she'd fallen asleep as soon as her head had touched the pillow, but now she was awake again, wondering, worrying.

The baby she was carrying was Nathan's, of course, but if she told him about her "miraculous" pregnancy, he'd no doubt explode with fury and he'd have every right.

For one thing, she'd told him she couldn't get pregnant and he'd believed her without question. It was the reason he hadn't bothered to use a condom any of the times they'd made love.

Damn him. Why *hadn't* he used a condom? For all he knew, she could have been a fortune hunter who had lied to him so that she could have his child. Once she'd told him she was pregnant, he might be angry with her, but if he wouldn't agree to marry her, he would most certainly agree to support his child. One way or another she would be set for life. Stupid man! How *dare* he put himself in that type of precarious situation.

She grabbed one of the pillows and threw it as far as she could. It landed in a pot of fringed irises. With a groan she fell back against the remaining pillows. There was no point in putting this off on him. *She* was the one who had been stupid.

And there were more reasons not to tell Nathan she was pregnant.

Protectively she laid her hand over her stomach. Dr. Robison had called this pregnancy a miracle, and it was. But there were no guarantees that another miracle could happen, and Nathan had said he wanted kids—*plural*.

Then there was the fact that Dr. Robison had asked her to cut out everything strenuous. To her that meant it was entirely possible she might lose the baby before she could bring it to term.

And something else too. Thanks to her, Nathan thought she and John were having an affair. Consequently Nathan would automatically think the baby was John's. Great. Just great.

As for herself, her hormones were running amok, carrying her spirits to dizzying heights of joy about the baby, then in the next moment sending her spiraling down toward confusions over what to do about Nathan, and always accompanied by buckets of tears.

Since the accident, she hadn't even been able to hope for a baby. She'd had to teach herself to accept this loss in her life and go on. In a way, her young students had become her children.

But now that the impossible had happened and a baby was actually growing inside her, she planned to do everything possible to bring this child to term.

As for Nathan? Perhaps it would be better if she didn't tell him at all.

"Nathan?"

Dani's lovely face swam into his mind's eye. It was the day of the picnic and she was laughing at his efforts at toe painting. *Picasso*, he'd said. *Maybe*, she'd responded. *When he was two years old*. And then she'd laughed again.

"Nathan?"

He felt a pen rap his knuckles and glanced around. *"What?"* He heard his sharp tone, then his mind snapped back to the present. He was in the soundproof conference room high in the Damaron Tower, where only blood members of his family were allowed. And with a few exceptions, all of his cousins were arrayed around the polished conference table, looking at him.

"Oh, good," Wyatt said with a grin. "You've joined us again."

"Sorry," he murmured. God, he was tired. If he could only get some sleep.

"Since you may have missed the decision that

was just made," Stephen said, "I'll repeat it. I'm going to Brussels instead of you."

"The hell you say."

Stephen nodded firmly. "Exactly. The hell I did say."

"I'm already packed," Nathan practically growled.

"My suitcases are being packed as we speak."

Nathan glared. Stephen smiled back at him.

Kylie, sitting to his left, slipped her hand over his. "You're not seeing what we're seeing, Nathan."

"What the hell is that supposed to mean?"

"There's something wrong with you. You've lost weight."

"And you've got circles under your eyes," Jonah added.

"In short, you don't look well at all," Sin finished.

"You're exaggerating. I'm fine, and I *will* go to Brussels as scheduled." He didn't honestly think he could forget Dani in Brussels, but at least there he'd be looking at different walls.

"It's Dani, isn't it?" Lion asked. "She's what's keeping you up at night and making you bite off our heads when we dare to say anything to you, even good morning."

Angrily he shoved back his chair and stood. "Mind your own damned business!"

"We are," Joanna said calmly from farther down the table. "You're a part of us and that makes anything or anyone that's upsetting you our business.

We've watched you for weeks now, waiting to see some sign that you've recovered from her, but you're only getting worse."

Wyatt nodded. "Which is why Stephen volunteered to go to Brussels and we decided to speak to you to see if we can help in some way, even if it's only to get you to talk about her."

"You know," Sin said, leaning back in his chair, his long legs propped atop the table. "We've all seen women this way over you, but we've never before seen you react this way about a woman. That's interesting, don't you think?"

"About as interesting as a train wreck." Nathan exhaled a long, steady breath. "Look, everyone. Dani was different, but I'll get over her. It's just a matter of time."

Yaz frowned. "Nathan, if it were only a matter of time, you would have gotten over her by now."

Nathan rubbed his face. He could yell, rant and rave, and even stalk out of the conference room, but he knew his cousins wouldn't be intimidated or deterred. On the opposite side of the coin, his cousins were the only people in the world from whom he'd take this prying into his life.

He sat back down. "You can't help and I can handle Brussels."

"Your business acumen is not what's in question," Kylie said.

"Why did you let her get away from you in the first place?" Lion asked.

Nathan shot him a killing look that made zero

impact. "She gave me no choice. There's someone else—someone she's known a lot longer than she's known me, someone she's in love with."

"So what?" Jonah asked.

"And you've just accepted the situation?" Wyatt asked.

"You all are not *listening* to me. Dani doesn't want me."

Sin swung his legs off the table, straightened, and pointed a finger at Nathan. "And you're not listening to *us*. Why aren't you at Dani's right now, trying to change her mind?"

Yaz shrugged. "Accepting no for an answer when it's something you really want is not like you at all, Nathan."

"What can I say?" he said slowly. Something had begun to niggle at him, something he should know, but it was at the edges of his mind, just out of his grasp. "You're right."

"Then what's different about Dani?"

"Different?" He gave a short laugh. "Just about everything."

"You've never been in love before, have you?" Yaz asked.

Nathan was silent for a moment. "You know I haven't."

"Has it occurred to you that *that's* what's different about Dani? That this time your heart is involved? That this time you've actually gone and fallen in love?"

"No . . . uh . . ." For the first time in weeks his vision began to clear.

"Think about it," Joanna said. "Sometimes love is confusing and you can't see what's right in front of your face. You were accustomed to having women act and react a certain way with you, and when Dani didn't, you were thrown. And then when finally she told you she had another lover, you backed off.

"I'm sure you were astounded that she'd chosen someone else over you, because it had never happened to you before. Secondly, it hurt you and made you angry and that further clouded the issue."

"And then there was the fact that you were in love with her," Yaz chimed in. "On some level maybe you wanted to respect her wishes. Maybe you even loved her so much, you wanted her to be happy. So you backed off."

"Which you shouldn't have," Jonah said. "Not if you want her, and I assume you do."

Nathan's hands slowly closed into fists. "Oh, I want her all right. I want her right here with me in hell."

"Great," Lion said with a big grin. "Then do something about it."

"I will," he said, his mind racing a mile a minute. "Just as soon as I clear this afternoon's schedule. And Stephen?"

"Yes?"

"Have a great time in Brussels."

———◆———————◆———

Dani had been to the Damaron Tower only twice before. On the day she and Nathan had visited Helene, he had whisked her into a private elevator that had taken them to the helipad. The return trip had reversed the process. As a guest of Nathan's on that day, doors were already open by the time she'd reached them.

But now she had come to the Tower as a normal person would, without the patronage of a Damaron. Smartly dressed people with purpose in their steps moved back and forth across the lobby, coming and going and appearing for all the world as if they knew exactly what they were doing.

They certainly had one up on her there, she reflected ruefully as she studied the enormous directory, looking for Nathan Damaron's name. But no specific Damaron name appeared. There were only a large number of the top floors that were marked as belonging to Damaron International.

Gazing at the directory, balancing on first one foot and then the other, she was left with the obvious conclusion that if a person wanted to conduct business with the Damarons, he or she needed an appointment and then they'd know where to go. Otherwise the Damarons didn't want you there.

She stood there, trying to decide what to do. She'd been afraid if she tried to call either Nathan or his office for an appointment, she would be turned down. And even if she'd somehow managed to get through to Nathan, she wouldn't have wanted to discuss the matter over the phone. So she'd decided to simply show up, no doubt the worst decision she could have made.

Yet again she felt overwhelmed at what she'd decided to do.

She'd come up with plenty of reasons not to tell Nathan and all of them were good reasons, true reasons. But even as she was coming up with them, she'd known the right thing to do.

Still, she'd struggled with herself for several days, agonizing over the decision. In the end, though, she'd finally had to admit that telling Nathan was the correct decision. She didn't have the right to keep such information from him. The man was going to be a father. He deserved to know.

She didn't even know if he was in town, but once she'd geared herself up to see him, she'd decided to act as quickly as possible. She wanted her confrontation with him to be over and done with.

Now all she had to do was find him.

In the end she chose the top floor of the block of floors that was marked as belonging to Damaron International. A minute later she was stepping off the elevator into a hushed, luxurious environment. She walked up to the first person she saw, a relatively young man wearing a serious expression and gold-rim glasses.

She drew in a deep breath, then hurried to speak before she backed out. "Excuse me, but I'm looking for Nathan Damaron." Her nervous voice cut through the silence, making her even more anxious.

"Do you have an appointment? All Damaron appointments wait on the floor below, then at the proper time they are escorted up here." The young man cast a quick glance around as if he expected to see another person, perhaps security.

"I didn't know that, but you see, I don't have an appointment."

"Then I'm sorry. The Damarons don't see anyone without an appointment." He walked over to the elevator from which she'd just departed and punched the button. "You need to make an appointment through the proper channels."

At that moment she'd have loved nothing more than to return home. For one thing, suddenly she wasn't feeling all that well. But she knew if she left, she'd never come back. "No, you don't understand. I need to see Nathan Damaron *now*. It's extremely important. If you could just tell him I'm here, I'm sure he'd want to see me." She didn't know anything of the sort, but in this case, she felt justified in bluffing. "My name is Danielle Savourat. I'm an . . . an acquaintance of his."

The young man eyed her as if trying to decide what category to put her in, and she didn't blame him. She knew she probably sounded crazy. She also knew she looked out of place. Her casual wardrobe possessed nothing she would consider smart or tailored, but she did keep a couple of outfits on hand for those times when she spent the weekend with her parents and went to church with them. For this visit, she'd chosen one of those outfits, a long, button-front dress with a princess line in black with tiny blue flowers on it. Because she'd lost weight, the dress hung loose on her, providing camouflage for her belly, which was just beginning to show.

"And what is your business with Mr. Nathan Damaron?"

"It's personal."

"I see. Well, I'm afraid Mr. Damaron is not available today." The elevator door opened and he stepped in, using his body to keep the door open. With a wave of his hand, he indicated she should enter.

"Not available?" She'd worked up her courage to come to see him and now he wasn't available? Her hope to get the meeting with him over as soon as possible crumbled. She felt incredibly disappointed and at the same time vastly relieved. Screwed-up hormones, again, she decided sourly. "What exactly does that mean? Is he here and busy with someone, or is he out of town?"

"I'm sorry, but I can't give you that information."

She tried to remain calm—getting upset wouldn't be good for the baby—but she could feel her frustration climbing, along with nausea and a light-headed feeling. "Look, I just want to see Nathan."

She was beginning to believe that she shouldn't have come here after all. But it was the right thing to do, she reminded herself, and more than anything else, she didn't want to have to make this trip again. So while she was here, she wanted to try everything possible to see Nathan. Then, if it didn't work out, she wouldn't blame herself. She took a deep breath and tried one more time.

"If you would just tell Nathan Damaron that Danielle Savourat needs to see him, I would be extremely grateful. I promise I won't take much of his time."

"Miss Savourat," the young man said firmly, "I will give your name to Mr. Damaron's assistant. After that, it will be up to Mr. Damaron as to whether or not he wishes to meet with you. In the meantime, if you don't willingly get on this elevator, I'm afraid I will have to call security."

Her heart sank. She'd known seeing Nathan might not be easy. Just because he'd freed up a lot of time for her when they'd been together didn't mean he'd automatically put himself at her disposal now. Besides, she was beginning to feel worse. The trip had taken more out of her than she had expected it would. The subway had been full and she'd had to stand all the way.

She should have taken a cab, but she was so used to riding the subway. Still, that was no excuse. She had to get used to the idea that she needed to think of the baby first. She'd definitely take a cab home. Her hand went to her stomach. *Hang in here with me, baby.* With a nod to the young man, she took a step toward the elevator.

"Dani?"

She swung around to find that Nathan had just walked up behind her, along with another man whom she didn't recognize, but who had a silver streak through his hair. Stupidly enough, Nathan's sudden appearance had caught her off guard.

Her heart beat wildly. Her mouth was surprisingly dry. She'd known she missed him, but she hadn't known how much until she'd turned around and seen him, his muscles tensed, his gray eyes dark and hard. The force of her pain mixed with her love for him had hit her hard and she had no defense against it. To make matters worse, she could detect no warmth or welcome in his gaze. "Nathan, I need to see you. Please. It's . . . important."

"I'm sorry, Mr. Damaron. I tried to tell her that you weren't—"

"It's all right, Mark." Nathan took Dani's arm, not gently. "I'll see you when you get back, Stephen. Dani, come with me."

His fingers bit into her arm as he ushered her into an office and closed the door behind them.

Pointing to a chair in front of a large desk, he released her. "Sit."

His abrupt tone left her feeling as if she'd been cut, but then after all, what had she expected? Weeks ago she'd hurt and confused him by insisting she didn't want to see him ever again, then added insult to injury by telling him she and another man were lovers. He was in a savage mood and she was the reason, and so for this short time she had to take his anger.

Still feeling light-headed and nauseous, she gratefully sank into the chair. But almost at once she was assaulted by his office, which was as over-powering as he was. The furniture was massive and made of dark woods. And it smelled of lemon oil, leather, and the dark spice scent of Nathan.

At that moment it seemed almost too much for her, and she thought she might pass out. She gripped the arms of the chair and tried to focus.

Settled behind his immense desk, he leaned his tensed body back in his chair. "I have to say, Dani, you're the last person I would have ever thought I'd see here at my office."

She clasped her hands together. "Yes, I know, and I appreciate your seeing me. I hope you know that I wouldn't have bothered you unless I had a very good reason."

"Just exactly how would I know that? As it turned out, I didn't really know you at all."

She swallowed, wishing she could ask him for a cup of tea to help with her nausea, but every line of his body shouted intractability. He didn't look well either. Too many late nights with beautiful women, she supposed, her heart aching.

"Despite how we parted, I never wanted to hurt you and I continue to want only the best for you."

"How very gracious of you." He hated her civility. He wanted to hurt her, to kiss her. . . . But it was all right, because she was here now. His anger was still a fire in his belly, but now he knew he loved her. He'd already given the instructions to clear his schedule for the afternoon, and she was going to stay until he figured out how he was going to win her back. But first he needed to know why she was here. He prayed it was because she and John had broken up and she wanted to reconcile with him.

"Nathan—"

"Why are you here, Dani? Did you come because you've decided it's me you want after all and you want us to get back together?"

She blinked. "No. I'm sorry if you received that impression, but—"

"Never mind." It had been too much to hope for. But, still, she was here. All he needed to do was work out some sort of strategy. That and try to ignore the hurt and anger in him that were growing by the second. "There's no need to apologize, Dani. I haven't exactly been pining away for you." What a stupid thing for him to say. But, God, the pain of simply holding himself back. She was so close. . . .

"Yes, I know. I've seen your picture in the papers with . . . different dates."

Good, he thought, allowing himself to feel the first satisfaction he'd felt in weeks. He'd hoped she would see those pictures. And since she had, it was worth the boring nights he'd had to spend to get them taken. After Dani, all other women had seemed vapid and colorless. "Okay, so what's the bottom line, Dani? Why are you here?"

"Yes, I should get straight to the point. I know you're a busy man." She cleared her throat, glanced down at her hands, then looked back up at him. "I came to tell you that I'm pregnant."

His gaze flew to where the material of her dress flowed over her stomach, then it lifted to her breasts and returned to her face. A charged silence filled the room while he stared at her, his mind for once blank. His heart was another matter, though. It felt as if it was breaking piece by piece.

"I have to say that you've surprised me once again." His voice was deliberately gruff to hide this new horrendous pain that was barely allowing him to breathe. "That was the last thing I expected you to say." *Wait.* There was a chance, just a chance, that the baby could be his. Wasn't there?

"I can only imagine what a shock this is for you. It was a shock for me too."

For safety, he retreated to sarcasm. "Naturally. Have you notified the media?"

"Excuse me?"

"You know. The tabloid newspapers and television programs."

"I'm afraid I don't understand."

"To alert them to be on the lookout for a new star in the east, of course." He shrugged. "After all, this, uh, pregnancy of yours certainly qualifies as an immaculate conception, since you led me to believe you couldn't get pregnant."

"I honestly didn't believe I could get pregnant. After the accident I was told that I was . . . so badly damaged and scarred that I would be unable to become pregnant, much less carry a baby. I was devastated." She put her hand protectively over her stomach.

He steepled his fingers together and for the first time noticed how pale she looked. She'd lost weight too. "So you're saying what? That the doctors were wrong?"

"At the time the doctors really believed what they told me, but as it turned out, even they couldn't predict a miracle."

"Very nice answer, Dani. You shift the blame to the doctors, then take it away."

"Nathan—"

The pain was choking him, but he congratulated himself on his calm facade. "What other lies have you told me?"

"Look, the only reason I came here today was to be up-front with you and tell you about the baby. If you don't choose to believe me, that's certainly your prerogative. But I *am* telling you the truth."

But she wasn't telling him what he was waiting to hear. Dammit, he was going to have to ask. He nodded his head in a formal gesture. "Then my congratulations to John. He must be very happy."

"John?"

"The proud papa—remember him? You told me you and he were lovers."

If possible, she went even paler. "That was a lie."

"Oh, *another* lie. So let's see. That makes lie

number two, doesn't it? How many others have you told me?"

"*None.* That is, I *did* let you believe that John and I were involved, something I'm not at all proud of. But it was the only way I could think of to get you to go away and leave me alone."

"Well, then, congratulations, Dani, because it certainly worked." If he'd been confused before, he was really confused now. She still wasn't saying that he was the father, yet why else would she come? To torment him some more? Or was there someone else other than John? God, he wasn't sure what to believe. Frustrated beyond endurance, he gave a hard shove to a heavy crystal paperweight, sending it skidding across his desk. It stopped right at the edge.

Tears threatened. Dani blinked them away. Her hand stayed firmly on her stomach. "Please, just listen. John and I have never been more than friends, but I thought it best for you to think we were involved."

"Oh, sure. I understand completely. There I was, an inch away from being a certified stalker, and you had to take drastic measures to get me to leave you alone."

"You weren't stalking me," she said sadly, fighting against the tears that kept threatening. Damn her for feeling sick right at this critical moment, she thought, looking around for something she could drink. Damn her hormones. And damn her lies that had gotten her into this mess. Truthfully, she'd lied to Nathan about John because she'd known if Nathan kept coming around, she'd give in to him. The irony now was that there was no longer any reason for her to keep him at arm's length, and now that there wasn't, he hated her.

She saw a pitcher of ice water, along with a set of crystal glasses sitting on a shelf. She carefully stood and made her way over to it in the hope that the cold water would help her nausea. Her hand shook as she lifted the pitcher. This encounter was taking far more out of her than she'd thought it would, far more out of her than was good for the baby.

Nathan's gaze, dark and stormy, stayed locked on her the whole time. "Your ploy worked perfectly, Dani. I stopped calling you and I stopped trying to see you. I gave up. So why are you here now, telling me that you and John *weren't* involved? You said you didn't want to get back together with me. So what's left?"

She set back down in the chair and took a sip of the water. "This is what's true, Nathan. I *did* believe I couldn't have a baby, and it *was* the reason I broke up with you. You told me you loved kids and I knew that in the long run a woman who couldn't have any would never be able to make you completely happy."

His eyes narrowed. "And just where did you get that little piece of information? Did *I* ever say anything like that? Did you even run your little theory by me?"

"No, but it was clear the day you helped me with the picnic. Remember? You said you definitely wanted to be a father one day and that you would like as many kids as possible."

"Most men I know feel that way at some time during their lives. At the same time some of them have to face that it's not going to happen. But they don't love their wife or the woman they're involved with any less. They either decide to stay childless or they look toward other options. But you didn't see fit to even give me that chance." His jaw clenched. "All on your own, you made the decision that you could never make me happy because you couldn't have kids. And then you drove me away. What absolute, one-hundred-percent garbage, Dani."

She set the water on the desk and wrapped her arms around herself. "It might seem incredibly stupid to you now, but at the time I thought I was doing the right thing."

"Stupid doesn't even come close to what I think about it. Dammit, Dani. What in the hell were you thinking? In the first place, we'd only known each other a short time by then. There was no thought of anything long-term between us, at least not on my part."

"You're right. There wasn't." By then she'd already fallen in love with him, but that was something she didn't want him to know. "It's just that I didn't want to stick around and see what happened. I decided the longer we were together, the more our inevitable parting would hurt." She swallowed against the rising nausea. "Nathan, try to put yourself in my position. That accident that Gil and I had was the greatest trauma of my life. It not only robbed me of Gil and our future, and the child I was carrying, it also, according to the doctors, robbed me of my chance of having babies. The accident might as well have torn my heart out, that's how devastated I was. I built a new life and I've been happy with it. But then you came along, and all I could think of was that sooner or later I was going to lose you too. You're right, it was a stupid thing to think at that point. But with everything I went through with the accident, I've never been exactly rational about the subject. If you wanted to have children, I wanted you to have every chance to have them."

"So the breakup was for *my* benefit?"

"In part." She reached for the water again and took another sip, but so far it wasn't making her feel any better. Right now the only thing she wanted to do was get out of his office without making a fool of herself by passing out.

"Don't you think I should have had some say in that decision?"

"If I'd brought it up, you would have thought I was crazy, because, as you said, we'd known each other such a short time."

"Maybe so, but at least I would have been informed. As it is, you didn't even give me a chance." He surged to his feet, crossed to the window, his hands balled into fists. "*Dammit*, Dani!"

While his back was turned, she swiped at a tear that was sliding down her face. "I'm not perfect, Nathan. Okay, so maybe I did mishandle things, but at the time it was the only way I knew to handle it. And now all I can say is that I'm sorry."

Slowly he turned back to her. "You're sorry. Okay, I've gotten that much. So let's get down to it, Dani. You've circled the subject, but you haven't yet said it. Who's the father of the baby?"

She started with surprise. "You don't know?"

"Tell me, dammit."

"You are. You. Nathan, I came here today because I wanted you to know that you're the father of my baby."

He stared at her. A vein throbbed in his temple and his fists were balled even tighter than they had been a minute ago.

"It's the *truth*, Nathan."

"And what kind of truth would that be, Dani? The kind of truth you told me when you said you and John were lovers? Or would it be the kind of truth you told me when you said you can't have a baby?"

She stood, too fast. The room whirled and she dropped back into the chair. Nausea rose to her throat. She sat perfectly still, willing it to go away.

Nathan frowned. "Are you all right?"

She took another sip of water, then nodded. "I'm fine. And I've said what I came here to say and now I have to go." Slowly, carefully, she stood again. Better. She'd already fainted once with this pregnancy. She had no plans to make it a second time, especially in front of Nathan.

"Don't you have something else to tell me?" he said, his voice low and raspy.

"What?" She racked her brain for something she'd forgotten, but all she could think of was how bad she was feeling. Mind over matter, she told herself. She was going to be fine.

"You haven't told me yet what you want."

"What I want?"

"Money," he prompted. "Aren't you going to ask me for money?"

She shook her head and immediately regretted it. The less movement the better. She really needed to leave. "No."

"Oh, come on, Dani. Think about it. I've seen the way you live. You must have thought about the money you could get out of me, the money that would allow you and your child to live in luxury."

She sighed. "Actually what I thought was that you were stupid for not using a condom no matter what I said, because I could have turned out to be a fortune hunter."

"And you were right. As it turned out, I was an imbecile for believing you. But in my defense, you were so hot that night, I would have had to be a damned statue not to want you right then and there."

"However," she went on, her voice shaking at the memory, "I'm not a fortune hunter, so you got off easy this time. Next time you should be more careful. And by the way, I love how I live. Now, if you'll excuse me, it's time for me to go."

"Not yet. Here's something else you should have thought about, Dani. If I decide to take you at your word that you really are carrying my baby, then there's no way I'm going to let you walk out that door."

She set the water glass on his desk. "Watch me." Such bravery, she reflected, when at the moment she wasn't even sure she could take a step.

"Face it, Dani. You took a chance by walking in here and telling me you're carrying my baby. If I choose, I could sue for complete custody. I have unlimited means, and by the time I got through with you, you'd only have the clothes on your back left."

"You do have the means, but no matter what you do, you won't get my baby."

"How do you figure that?"

"Because to get my baby, Nathan, you'd have to kill me, and for all your power and wealth, when push came to shove, I don't believe you would do that. So cut out the threats. I came here to tell you about the baby, because I thought you had a right to know, and now I've done that. If in the future you'd like to have something to do with your child, then I'll be glad to work out what I consider a reasonable visitation schedule."

"Reasonable visitation?" He came around the desk, hitched his hip on its corner, and glared at her. "What you really mean is you're going to try to dictate to me when I can and can't see my child."

Sitting down would be a really good thing for her to do right about now, but he was entirely too close to the chair. She regarded him, thinking. Maybe it was because she was feeling really awful. Or maybe it was because he'd just put her through the wringer. But she couldn't resist a dig. "Why worry about it now? Who knows? Maybe I *have* lied to you again, and the baby will turn out to be John's after all. Just think how convenient that will be since we live right across the hall from each other."

"Sorry, but that won't work."

"Living across the hall from each other?"

"Trying to pass the baby off as John's if it's not. I'll be able to tell at a glance whether the child is mine or not."

She eyed his silver streak with a wry smile. "Of course you will. How strange that I didn't think about that. Good-bye, Nathan." She took two steps, then suddenly lunged for the wastebasket by his desk.

"Dani—"

She threw up and there wasn't a thing ladylike about her actions. The little bit she'd had for breakfast, along with what she'd managed for lunch, emptied into the elegant leather wastebasket, ruining it for all time.

"For God's sake, Dani," she heard Nathan say. "Why didn't you tell me you weren't feeling well?"

She felt his arm around her and his hand supporting her forehead.

When the convulsions subsided, he handed her a handkerchief. Gratefully she wiped her mouth with it. "I'm sorry."

"Don't be ridiculous." Holding her against him, he half carried her into a room off the office that turned out to be a bathroom suite. "Here." He pulled open a drawer that had several new toothbrushes still in their package, along with several tubes of toothpaste. Then he opened a cabinet and pointed out fresh towels and washcloths. "Would you like me to stay? Do you need my help?"

She shook her head, embarrassed that he'd seen her in such a vulnerable moment.

"Then I'll be right outside. If you need something, call. Okay?"

She nodded and waited for him to shut the door. When she was finally alone, she leaned heavily against the sink. "Damn," she whispered. She'd tried everything she could think of to hold herself together in front of Nathan, but in the end she hadn't been able to. So now all she could do was to get out of his office with as little fuss and exertion as possible.

TEN

When Dani returned to Nathan's office, she found him sitting on the edge of his desk, writing on a yellow legal pad propped on his knee.

When he heard her come out of the bathroom, he looked up, his eyes filled with concern. "Does that sort of thing happen often?"

"Sometimes, but usually in the morning. I guess taking the subway here wasn't the best idea. It was so crowded and the smells—"

"You took the *subway*?"

"I always take the subway."

"That habit just stopped," he said firmly. "I'm taking you home in my car."

"Oh, no—"

"What soothes your stomach?"

"Excuse me?" Her mind was still fixed on the idea of Nathan taking her home. The last thing she needed today was to have to spend more time alone with him.

"For your nausea," he prompted. "What makes it better?"

Throwing up had helped a lot, she thought irreverently. "Crackers and tea, sometimes soda, but—"

He grabbed the phone and punched in a number. "Have my car ready and stock it with crackers, soda, and tea. Thanks." He dropped the receiver back into its cradle. "By the time we get downstairs, everything will be ready." He resumed writing, his hand quickly moving back and forth across the page.

Momentarily fascinated, she stared at the phone, wondering who worked for him that could make tea that fast. "Look, Nathan. You're right. I'm not up to riding the subway home and I'd already planned to take a cab. So I'll take you up on the offer of your car with thanks. But you don't have to come with me. I'm sure you have a very busy afternoon. I can go home alone and I'll be perfectly fine."

He didn't look up. "Then you're feeling better?"

"Yes."

"That's good to know."

"Okay, I'll be going." Relieved that he wasn't fighting her on the issue of her going home alone, she started for the door. "Thank you again for the use of your car."

"Just a second."

She looked back. "What?"

He threw his pen on the desk and tore off the page. "Okay, now I'm ready. Let's go."

"I told you—"

He cut her off. "We have things to talk about, Dani." Outside his office, he handed the long yellow sheet of paper to an older, well-dressed woman who seemed to have been waiting for him. "My instructions are all there. If an emergency comes up, you know how to get me."

"Yes, Mr. Damaron."

The next thing Dani knew, she was on a different elevator than the one she'd ridden to reach his floor, and it was descending at lightning speed. "Ohhh." Automatically her hand reached out to cover her stomach.

"Dani?"

She shook her head, knowing that if she spoke, she'd probably throw up again. On the other hand, her stomach would have to catch up with her first and it was still on an upper floor.

"Sorry," he murmured. He stepped closer and put his arm around her for support. "Just hang on."

When the elevator doors parted to reveal a garage, he swooped her up in his arms and carried her to a long black limousine, where his driver waited with the rear door open. A minute later she was comfortably settled, with a tray containing a cup of hot tea and a plate of crackers by her side, and the car was pulling out into the traffic.

The speed and efficiency with which Nathan

moved left her dazed, and suddenly she became aware of how tired she was.

Sometime during the drive home, Dani fell asleep, and when she awoke she found herself in her own bed. Stunned, she lay there for a moment, trying to figure out what had happened. Never before had she fallen so deeply asleep that she wouldn't have awakened if someone had lifted her out of a car and carried her into her apartment. She lay there for a moment, trying to orient herself. There was an enticing smell coming from her kitchen, and she thought she heard the low murmuring of a male voice. Nathan. He was still here. With a groan she slid off the bed.

Fifteen minutes later, after showering and changing into jeans and a T-shirt, she made her way into her living room. Nathan was there, talking quietly on his cell phone.

His carefully folded jacket lay over the back of a chair. The top buttons of his shirt were undone, his tie hung loose around his neck, and his sleeves were unbuttoned and rolled up. A laptop computer rested on his thighs and his cell phone was cradled between his cheek and shoulder.

As soon as he saw her, he hit a series of computer keys and spoke into the phone. "Okay, Yaz. Talk to you soon." He pushed the disconnect button.

"Hi," he said, closing up the computer and setting it aside. "Are you feeling better?"

"Much better, thank you, but you didn't have to hang up on your call."

"My cousin and I were just going over some numbers for a project, but we'd finished."

Yaz—his beautiful cousin Yasmine, she translated to herself, the one she'd seen with him at their charity ball. She remembered wondering what it would be like to be the recipient of such uncensored warmth and genuine, uncomplicated love from him. She still wondered.

"Why didn't you wake me up when we arrived here?"

He smiled. "You were out cold. You obviously needed the rest."

There was no disputing that. She'd spent most of the last few nights wrestling over the decision of whether or not to tell him about the baby. "Still, there was no reason for you to stay."

"There was every reason. Earlier today you told me you were having my baby. In my book that means we have a great deal to talk about."

She stifled a sigh. "I don't want to argue with you again."

"We're not going to argue. We're going to *discuss*. But first, you should try to eat something. You must be hungry."

"I am. What is that wonderful smell?"

"As far as I can tell, it seems to be a chicken consommé."

"John?"

A muscle flexed in his jaw. "Chances are good, since I found it in your refrigerator. At any rate, it looked nourishing. I decided to heat it up and have it ready for you when you woke."

"Thank you. Would you like a bowl of it too?"

"No," he said, getting to his feet. "My driver brought me in some takeout a couple of hours ago, but sit down and I'll serve you."

She shook her head. "I don't need you to wait on me."

"Maybe not, but I'm going to. Is there anything else I can get you while I'm at it?"

She sighed. "Crackers and a soda, please."

"I'll be right back."

True to his word, he quickly returned with a tray containing a large bowl of the consommé, a stack of crackers, and a soda. "Wonderful," she said sometime later. "I was really hungry."

"I'm not surprised. There couldn't have been anything left in your stomach."

She almost groaned at the reminder of what had happened at his office. "I'm really sorry about your wastebasket."

"Forget it. I'm sure it's already been replaced." He paused. "Do you think the consommé will stay down?"

She smiled wryly. "I hope so, but there are no guarantees."

With a nod, he took the tray and returned it to

the kitchen. Back in her living room, he chose a chair at a right angle to the one she was sitting in.

"Okay, Dani," he said, shifting his body toward her. "I want to explain a few things to you, not the least of which is why I acted like a complete jackass when you showed up in my office."

"No. There's no need. I understand. I lied and hurt you. You hurt me back."

"You got it in a nutshell."

She shook her head in sadness. "There's no point in going over it again."

"Please—I need to tell you some things—to explain a little more."

He wasn't going to back down. She could see the determination in his eyes. Reluctantly she nodded.

"I've nearly gone mad without you, Dani." He gave a shaky laugh. "And that's no exaggeration—just ask my cousins. Images of you and John . . ." He closed his eyes. "The anger, the pain—they've been eating me alive. Truthfully, it was probably only a matter of time before I came looking for you."

"What for?" she asked ruefully. "To kill me?"

He smiled slightly. "I might have been tempted, but I would have been too busy trying to win you back. Just like I'm doing now."

Her heart skipped a beat. What was he saying?

"But then you showed up today and caught me at a moment when there was a lot going on with me. My cousins had just made me realize something that had thrown me off balance. Then right afterward you were there, and I was ecstatic."

"That was ecstasy?"

He grinned. "Yeah, and anger and pain. And you got the brunt of the last two. Finally I had the opportunity to try to make you pay for the way you had hurt me."

"You had every right."

"I thought I did, but I was wrong. And I *am* sorry, Dani. Physically you weren't up to it."

"You didn't know that."

"I would have if I'd paused long enough to think about it. I noticed you were pale and had lost weight, but I didn't stop and—"

"It's over and done with, and I'm the one who should be sorry and I am." She shrugged. "I can't even say we're even. I hurt you when I told you I was having an affair with John and you didn't deserve to be hurt. Then you hurt me when you didn't believe the baby was yours and I *did* deserve to be hurt. After all, my lie was the reason you didn't believe me in the first place."

"Let's try something new," he said softly. "Let's stop assigning blame. From this moment on I want us to forget the past and go forward."

She slowly shook her head. "I'm not sure that can be done. I made some really stupid decisions, Nathan, and I know it. And if tomorrow you and I were in the same position again, I'd probably do the same thing."

He stared at her for a moment. "That accident

did more than scar your body, it scarred your heart. I know that now. I also know how hard it must have been for you to come to me today. But thankfully you did."

"It was the right thing to do."

"Yes, it was. You can't even begin to know how grateful I am that you did. And we have a lot more to talk about, but right now I want to know exactly what your doctor has said about your pregnancy."

"Why?" she asked carefully. "What difference does it make to you?"

"Because you're carrying my baby and I'm very concerned about you."

"You really do believe me." She hadn't been completely, one hundred percent sure until that moment. A heaviness in her heart lifted.

"I believe you," he said softly. "Now tell me what the doctor said."

"That this could be a very difficult pregnancy."

"*Could* be?"

She nodded. "First of all, the nausea means nothing. That's normal. Even the light-headedness is normal under certain circumstances."

His brow rose. "What light-headedness?"

"I've fainted once and come close several other times."

"Dammit, Dani. Why didn't you come to me sooner?"

She almost laughed. "Why? Could you have kept me from fainting?"

"Maybe."

"Even *you* aren't that powerful."

"No, but I could have been there to catch you."

For the first time in days she smiled. "He also said that I'm going to have to start moderating my activities. As much as I'm going to hate it, I'll probably have to sit while I teach my classes. It's going to make teaching infinitely harder, but I have friends—dancers—who may not mind coming in to help me from time to time."

"What about just *stopping* the classes?"

"I don't want to do that if at all possible. But if I have to I will. I'm willing to do any and everything I can to carry this baby to term."

"Including allowing me to help you?"

She eyed him uncertainly. "Would you want to? Can you really forget the awful things I've said to you? Can you *honestly* forget them?"

"We're starting over, remember? And it's time I told you some of my truths now. Remember when I said my cousins made me realize something today?" He laughed a little. "I guess it was a Damaron version of an intervention. But it worked. They made me realize something I hadn't even come close to guessing."

"What?"

"That I love you. That I can't live without you. That I want you by my side all the days of my life."

"You—?"

"I love you more than you'll ever be able to know, Dani. It was the reason I couldn't let go of my pain and anger—I couldn't let *you* go."

Her heart stopped. Her breath caught in her throat. Speech deserted her.

His smile was gentle. "Are you really that surprised?"

Numbly she nodded.

He reached for her hand. "Believe me, when I finally realized it, I was too. And then you showed up and told me you were pregnant. My first thought was that the baby was John's, but my second was that I hoped like hell it was mine." His eyes filled with tears. "Then when you told me it was, I was so damned happy, not only because of the baby, but because it would mean you'd be back in my life again. But at the same time I realized something else—that even if the baby you were carrying was someone else's, I didn't care. Either way, I realized that I loved you and I wanted you in my life forever."

Her heart filled with joy. In her wildest imaginings she couldn't have predicted his response. "Do you mean that?"

He slid off the chair, knelt in front of her, and reached for her hand. "More than I've ever meant anything in my life. And there's one more thing. While I was waiting for you to wake up this afternoon, I realized that there's a possibility you love me. You may not even know it yet." She opened her mouth to tell him he was right, but he held up his hand. "Just keep an open mind for a minute. See, here's the thing. You said you broke up with me because you knew that someday I'd want children and you thought you couldn't give them to me. That means you were putting my well-being above your own. And guess what? That's part of the definition of love. Or maybe you just didn't care about me and were using that as an excuse. But either way it doesn't matter, because I love you and I'm not going anywhere. For better or worse and for the rest of your life, when you look around, I'll be there right by your side."

"Thank God," she murmured, tears of happiness beginning to slide down her face, "because I *do* love you, more than I can say." She wiped away her tears. "But before we say anything more, there's something you should know. There's a possibility I may not be able to carry this baby to term. And even if I do, I may never be able to conceive again."

He frowned. "Do you *still* think that matters to me? Haven't I convinced you yet how much I love you? Dani, *you're* what counts. You're the *only* thing that counts. If we never have a child, I'll still be deliriously happy because I have you."

"Do you honestly mean that?"

"With all my heart." He stood, gently lifted her from the chair, then sat back down with her on his lap. "I don't ever want to be without you again. *Ever.* Please say you'll marry me."

Seven Months Later
Dani shifted her sleeping newborn baby in her

arms. "I can't put him down," she murmured. "He's so beautiful."

Nathan eased down on the bed beside her. "The only thing I've ever seen more beautiful than he is you."

Her heart swelled with joy and she leaned her head back on the pillow and smiled up at her husband. "I haven't looked in a mirror yet, but I can imagine how awful I look."

"Didn't you just hear me? I've never seen you look more beautiful."

"Thank you. After nine hours of labor I think I deserve that lie."

He chuckled. "It's not a lie, sweetheart. You take my breath away with your beauty and your strength. I honestly don't know how I got so lucky to have you in my life." His eyes moistened. "If I haven't said it before, I should say it now. Thank you for choosing me to kiss on that Paris quay. And while I'm at it, thank you for all the sickness you went through and the bed time you had to endure in order to bring our son into our world."

"There's nothing I wouldn't have done or endured to have him." She was so happy she was sure she was beaming.

"You may have won the prize in Paris, but now that I have you two, I've definitely won the biggest prize of all."

Mischief entered her misty blue eyes. "And you know what that means?"

"What, honey?"

"It means that now *you* owe *me*."

He laughed heartily, but the sleeping baby in his wife's arms didn't even stir. His heart was more full of love than he'd ever thought possible. "I'll do anything, *anything*, in the world for you. What do you want?"

"Really? You'll do anything for me?"

He nodded. "Absolutely."

"Then kiss me as if you're madly in love with me and are never going to let me go."

He smiled down at her. "Piece of cake."

THE EDITOR'S CORNER

With these, our last LOVESWEPTs, so many thanks are in order, it's impossible to know where to start. I feel a little like those people at awards ceremonies—afraid of leaving someone off the "thank you" list.

It goes without saying that we owe our biggest thanks to the authors whose creativity, talent, and dedication set LOVESWEPT apart. As readers, you've experienced firsthand the pleasure they brought through their extraordinary writing. . . . Love stories we'll never forget, by authors we'll always remember. Nine hundred and seventeen "keepers."

Our staff underwent a few changes over the years, but one thing remained the same—our commitment to the highest standards, to a tradition of innovation and quality. Thanks go out to those who had a hand in carrying on that tradition: Carolyn Nichols, Nita Taublib, Elizabeth Barrett, Beth de Guzman, Shauna Summers, Barbara Alpert, Beverly Leung, Wendy McCurdy, Cassie Goddard, Stephanie Kip, Wendy Chen, Kara Cesare, Gina Wachtel, Carrie Feron, Tom Kleh, and David Underwood.

Special thanks go to Joy Abella. Joy often said that being an editor for LOVESWEPT was her dream job and not many people got to realize their dreams. Thanks, Joy, for helping us realize how lucky we all were to have been a part of this remarkable project. ☺

Finally, thank you, the readers, for sharing your thoughts and opinions with us. Fifteen years of LOVESWEPTs was possible only because of your loyalty and faith. We hope you will continue to look for books by your favorite authors, whom you've come to know as friends, as they move on in their writing careers. I'm sure you'll agree they are destined for great things.

With warm wishes and the hope that romance will always be a part of your lives,

Susann Brailey

Susann Brailey

Senior Editor